E. S. Ready

Until Someday

Copyright © 2016 by E.S. Ready

First Printing – July 2016

Cover Illustration/Design © 2016 by Veronica Ready, Tori Ready

This novel is a work of fiction. The characters, names and incidents portrayed within are solely the work of the author's imagination. Any resemblance to actual persons, living or dead, localities or events is entirely coincidental.

Published in the United States of America

ISBN-13: 978-1534884090

ISBN-10: 1534884092

Special thanks to my editor, Sarah, for helping me make this book what it is.

My youngest sister, Marlee, for reading the very first draft of *Until Someday* and everything I write. Thank you for being my #1 fan.

My mother, Veronica, and my sister, Tori. Thank you both for your attention to detail and making the cover of this book perfect.

My father, Scott, the hardest working man I'll ever know.

All the family and friends who read this story and will read whatever I come up with next. I appreciate your support.
I love you all.


*SO* – You made me a writer.

IV

For my grandmother and friend, Angela.

Thank you for my appreciation of stories.

We miss you, we love you.


P.S. – Thanks for the postcard.

# UNTIL SOMEDAY

*An Emmett Roane Story*

# E. S. READY

"The real man can smile in trouble, can gather strength from distress, and grow brave by reflection. 'Tis the business of little minds to shrink, but he whose heart is firm, and whose conscience approves his conduct, will pursue his principles unto death."

- Thomas Paine

# 1.

Thursday, November 17th, 1927

I'm looking at the ocean, my feet upon some unknown beach in a timeless time. The salty breeze finds its way into the cracks of my life, stinging some parts while simply awakening others. My eyes blink slowly, focusing, searching for clues. The whitecaps wink back at me before they crash and die. I eventually find what I am looking for, first one footprint, and then another. There are many of them in the wet grain of the coast. My careful eyes admire the small imprints, one in front of the next, leading into the sea and probably beyond. I follow the trail for however long – I don't really know. I release a hope and a prayer that those footprints are yours.

I write letters to you in my mind. Sometimes they are mailed out in daydreams, sometimes in nightmares. Sometimes they don't go anywhere at all. They stay between my ears in a pool of memories that somehow fades and replenishes simultaneously and miraculously like the waves. It defies all logic, Anna.

I miss you. I love you, still.

You could have at least sent me a postcard from wherever you are.

The surf gradually becomes louder, shouting at me like horizontal rain. I realize before it's too late that there is no surf, no sand. The hammering is that of a crowd. People, so many people, screaming into my square space of violence.

I'm on my back on the canvas floor of a boxing ring. The last punch that whatever-his-name landed on the left side of my face put me here. I see a bright light above me. *Perhaps I'm dying or dead. No, that would be far too easy.*

A man in a white shirt and a black tie stands over me. His neatly combed hair falls slightly out of place in front as his arm swings downward, pointer finger extended. He's yelling something over the noise of the crowd. *My oh my, he's dressed nice for a fighter. Wait, he's not a fighter. He's the goddamn referee and he's shouting at me.*

"Two! Three!"

Sound has now come back to me, unfortunately at full volume. The noise in the arena drives a railroad tie of pain into my skull. I wish this chump had knocked me out completely. Seriously.

"Emmett!" Someone close by yells. "Emmett!"

My head swivels in the direction of a male voice. It's Brian, my manager, trainer, and friend. "Emmett!" His hands are cupped at the sides of his mouth to amplify his voice. *Emmett? Is that my name? That is my name, right? My first name is Emmett. How hard did this boob of a boxer hit me?*

"Four! Five!"

I do remember the boob's name: Earl "Curly" McKlellen. "Curly" on account of his hair, which looks a lot like the tuft of a clown, but dames love it. Right now the clown is looking pretty cocky. I managed to kick his sly ass twice before, but now Mr. Curls feels that his revenge has been had. Now I'm glad he *didn't* knock me out because I intend to mop that smile off his face so hard he wont be able to wipe himself later on. As soon as

I decide to get up. Perhaps I'll take a catnap first.

"Six! Seven!" The ref startles me.

"Emmett!" Brian screams desperately as my vision becomes clearer.

Brian's blonde hair and high shoulders come into view as he whips a towel onto the canvas in front of him. He's angry; well, so am I. This fight was even until a lucky punch found its way to me.

"Get the fuck up, Emmett! Now, you putz!"

I try to move, but can't.

"Eight!"

My head turns in the opposite direction and I search for you. You always wear an outrageous hat so that I can spot you easily. My vision flickers.

Where are you, Anna?

For a moment I swear I see your face in the crowd, beyond the hats and hands in the air, beyond the cigar smoke. You aren't wearing one of your hats, though. Your long brown hair flows over your shoulders. You never wear makeup because you don't need to, only the expensive lipstick I bought you. The color is a little too bright but you wear it anyway because you know it makes me smile. I would smile regardless. I can't hear you, but I can read those beautiful lips.

"Get up, Emmett."

"I'm trying," I reply.

"Please…"

My shoulders leave the canvas. I'm rising.

"Nine!"

I'm on my feet and the crowd erupts in cheers.

McKlellen faces the crowd, nodding his head and waving his gloves in the air. He thinks the crowd is cheering for him. My stance is unstable, but I am standing nonetheless.

"Turn around, Curly." I say as I spit blood onto the spot that moments ago served as my temporary bed.

As he turns around, a look of disbelief settles on his face. His features are more discolored and pummeled than mine.

He says, "You should have stayed down, Roane." *Roane... I knew my last name started with an R.*

I motion him toward me, taunting him.

"Don't miss me," I say.

"I didn't!" he snarls, smiling at the sight of me wobbling toward him.

*At least if I go down I'll appear brave. To hell with bravery... I've had enough of bravery. Please let me land a good one before he has the chance again.*

He charges at me like a Comanche, his fists alternating high and low at my body. I block most of his shots. The two blows that I fail to derail bounce off my flexed stomach. He winds up again and I can feel his knuckles through the gloves as he throws everything he has at me. I raise my arms higher to stop the attack from inflicting true damage to my face.

My turn.

I hit him the same way he hit me. The difference is that my punches, blocked or not, rattle his descendants. I somehow saved this explosion of firepower and I smack him around the ring like a limp ragdoll. The crowd is nearly out of control. I am fueled by its raw energy.

McKlellen manages to land a couple of decent shots before running out of steam. He's tired, more than I am now, and I'm as glad as a pig in shit for that. We go back and forth, shot for shot, for maybe two minutes. It feels more like two hours.

Finally, I have him against the ropes and unleash another furious barrage that he cannot contend with. All that I have left in me is launched at him. If this doesn't work, this fight will be a draw, or worse, a humiliating defeat.

More likely a defeat.

I connect twenty or twenty-five jabs to his stomach, ribs and both sides of his curly head. His defenses crumble and I take a step back, my right hand cocked back as if to release an arrow from a bow. I throw a haymaker and McKlellen drops backwards onto the same canvas I lay fading on just minutes before. The count is on. I allow my eyes three seconds to scan the crowd for you. Where are you? You have escaped me again, Anna.

As the numbers ascend to ten I walk coolly around the ring in an effort to decompress myself. I look at Brian, my downed opponent, and back to Brian.

I don't gloat, I don't grin. Well, maybe a little.

McKlellen doesn't come to his feet for some time. He lies in the ring motionless. Eventually he stirs and shifts onto his side. *At least I didn't kill him.* His people chaotically climb into the ring to render him aid as the referee raises my hand to declare me the winner. Brian and several others from my corner duck under the ropes to congratulate me, throwing my dark purple robe on my weary shoulders. I am grateful for the cold canteen of water. They gather around me in a semi-huddle.

I say to them, "If we don't get the hell out of here now, I may be down for the count, whether this fight is over or not."

Brian nods at my exhaustion and wipes my face with the same towel he had been agitatedly smacking into the canvas just moments ago. "Let's go, pally," he says.

We exited the ring as fast as we could amidst the mobs of intoxicated people. Whether they were drunk from illegal booze or the excitement from the fight or both, it didn't matter to me – I just wanted to leave. Somewhere beyond the mounds of spectators I heard the crashing of a band. Camera bulbs flashed in my direction, the white light sticking into my brain, mimicking thumb tacks. Normally I would have taken the time to shake a couple of hands, sign a couple of gloves, and kiss a couple of dames. One time I shook hands with J.D. Rockefeller. The magnate was so old that I feared crushing his hand. There would be no shaking of hands today, no kissing of dames, no J.D. Rockefeller.

Thank Christ for cops. An officer parted the sea of people like a uniformed Moses and before long I was out of sight. The tunnel that led to my locker room was dark, cold and welcoming.

# 2.

Brian and the others remained outside the door, conversing with a reporter, a cop, and some swanky sap. The locker room, to my pleasure, was dimly lit since Brian had seen to it that half the bulbs were loosened prior to my arrival. The space around me was chilled, and the air clung to my sweat as I moved like a ghost beside the long bench, my robe floating over the floor. I stepped up to the sink and examined my face in the cracked mirror, a mirror that had been fine before I punched it a couple of weeks ago after losing a match that I should have had in the bag.

My features were still sharp, despite being hit so many times: the typical marks and scrapes but no serious cuts or bruises. "Your jawline looks like it's made out of granite," Anna would say. "That doesn't mean it *is* granite. Keep it protected so that you can use it and I can keep feeding you." She would run her finger up my jaw and over the scar on my right temple. That scar... a reminder that a bullet has the potential to end your life much faster than a punch. Some fucking Hun almost had me that day. That day, in a separate and far more horrific war than the one I fought in boxing rings. I was eighteen then, a child. A decade ago that on some days feels like yesterday. Sometimes I consider growing my hair longer instead of leaving it shaved close on the sides. *Why hide the scar?* I inevitably ask my twenty-seven-year-old reflection. *Leave it as a reminder.*

Lately I find myself wishing that perhaps that bullet had been on target instead of a graze. She would have never had a scar to run her delicate finger over because I would have ceased to exist. I would have been spared the pain of losing her.

My parents, the cornerstones of my life, have stopped coming to my fights. They can't bear to watch the shit get knocked out of me anymore. Most Sundays I still visit them for dinner. My father is Irish and my mother Italian and I surmise that explains both my fair skin coupled with a greater than average amount of body hair. It may also explain my love for alcohol, food, and of course, fighting.

My eyes have grown darker over the years, if that's even possible. What was once a lighter blue is now a deeper blue, almost to the point of becoming a purple tone that matches my boxing robe. My hair is usually parted to the right side and kept like a gentlemen on days that I decide to give a crap. The dark brown of my hair is made darker by the application of Dapper Dan pomade, the only pomade I use, to hell with the rest. I've been told I should act in shows or pictures. I don't really go to shows or pictures but I'm going to go right ahead and assume, for my sake, that that means I'm a good-looking fellow.

If the day comes, perhaps where I can't box, which it eventually will, I can be an actor. I'll request a minimal amount of lines and get away with standing there like a fucking dunce, living the dream surrounded by famous people and loose flappers.

That'll be the day, I tell ya.

At a whopping one hundred and seventy-three pounds, I'm a middle-weight fighter. I've managed to keep that weight for the better part of the last decade. My build is muscular and I suppose I'm a stitch stronger than most men who stand at five feet, eight inches tall.

I felt like punching that mirror again for some reason. I didn't like the way this guy was staring back at me through those dark, deep-set eyes. There was a knock on the door.

"You don't have to knock, you know," I said.

Brian entered alone, the look on his face melancholy.

"What happened out there, Emmett?"

I continued staring at the man in the mirror.

"What do you mean *what happened?*" I asked. "I beat him."

"You almost didn't this time. Last time, two weeks ago, that was a reality. You put on a show tonight, kid, but…"

"But what?"

"But you're slipping. Curly is a palooka. You should have smoked him in the first round."

I considered hashing it out with him but there was no fight left in me. Brian was like a brother. He knew what I knew, and what I knew wasn't good. "Yes, I am," I said.

The expression on his face showed his surprise at my fold into honesty.

"I am slipping," I began unwrapping my hands.

"Is it because of *her?*" he asked.

I walked away from both him and my own reflection and yanked my locker open. My eyes traveled up the spine of F. Scott Fitzgerald's *The Great Gatsby*, Ernest Hemingway's *The Sun Also Rises*, William Shakespeare's *Macbeth*, and a book about ancient Rome. The flask rested on my clothes. The stainless steel gleamed, even in the soft light of the room. I picked it up and looked at the engraved initials "E.S.R." The flask easily found its way to my lips. Liquor slid down my throat before creating a small comforting fire in the pit of my stomach.

Gin… that scent of pine, like a Christmas tree. Just a few sips of it brought me back to that holiday, the last holiday I had with her before the script flipped and life played a dirty trick on me.

I'm sitting with you, Anna, on the couch in the small living room of my parents' home. The radiator hisses at us, like a jealous rival. The time is late enough for Christmas Eve to be confused with Christmas. The delightful smell of my mother's cooking lingers as the rest of the party migrates to the kitchen, where I can hear my sister holding court amongst laughter. Both the radio and the fire are low enough for me to almost hear your thoughts as you give me your gaze. Your eyes are a better blue than mine, like two skies forever cloudless.

"You look at me as if I'm a thousand miles away," I say to you. "I'm right here."

"I know that," you reply. Your eyebrows lift with both corners of your lips. "I'm trying to read your mind, tough guy."

"Oh, is that so?"

"'Tis so."

"Like when we were kids?"

"Just like when we were kids." Your smile grows; such a thing it is.

"And what is it you see, love?" I ask, my voice low.

"I'm not quite as good as I was back then. You have your guard up again." The index finger of your left hand traverses the scar above my ear, underlining your sentence.

I say, "You're a funny bird for thinking you have to out-fox my guard. You're in there already," I tap my forehead, "farther than anyone and probably for a lifetime."

"Is that so?" you ask.

"'Tis so, Anna."

10

"When you say my name it makes me blush. You know I hate it." You're right. I can see roses on your cheeks.

"Get used to it, Anna."

"Fine, Emmett."

"What am I thinking about now?"

"You're thinking about... kissing me."

"Well... you're not wrong," I say and lean in.

You do the same and your lips meet mine with a brushstroke and a grasp. Eventually we retreat, overwhelmed, our faces inches away from each other. You are radiant, your features outlined by brown hair that acts as a polished wood frame.

You find words before I do and say, "Oh, I almost forgot your gift!"

"I told you not to get me anything."

"Well, why would I listen to you?"

"Because I'm your fiancé?" I smile.

"I have many fiancés, you just don't know about them." You laugh and lean over the arm of the sofa. When you turn back to me you're holding two small, wrapped boxes, one in each hand.

"I'm clearly your favorite," I joust.

"Now you're reading *my* mind," you say.

"Which one do I open first?"

"This one." You hold up the one in your left hand. "No, this one." You switch to the right hand. "Oh jeez, it doesn't matter – either."

"You spoil me." I pick the one in your left palm. The wrapping tears slowly under my fingers, revealing a cigar box.

"Rolled in Connecticut," I say as I open the lid and smell the tobacco. "My favorite."

"I know," you say. "Now open the other. You saved the better of the two for last and you didn't even know it."

I take the second gift and remove the paper from it. It's another small wooden box. "More cigars?"

"Better," you assure.

I slide open the lid and find a stainless steel flask. My thumb runs over the monogram of my name before pulling it from its packaging. "This is beautiful." I admire it for a long moment before turning back to you. "Thank you."

"Engraved it myself," you tell me.

"I believe it," I say with another kiss. "Marvelous, really."

My hand sinks into the couch cushion where I stashed your gift. I present it to you: a small covered box no bigger than my palm.

"Emmett, what is this?" Your bright eyes dart from the gift and back up to me. "I told you not to get me anything, especially after all you spent on the ring."

"And why would I listen to you?" I play.

You move your shoulders in a bashful way.

"Go on, Anna, before I give it away to another dame."

"Fat chance in hell, love." You take the box, undress it, and pop it open.

The necklace inside is a silver key with a heart on the end. Your lower lip trembles until it's met with your fingertips.

"How did you know?" You take it from the case. "I always wanted one of these."

"Lucky guess. Lucky guess from a lucky guy."

You attach it around your neck and center the key over your heart. "It's really something, truly."

"You're really something."

"I feel bad now. Here you got me something sweet and all I got you were things to put you three sheets to the wind."

"Nonsense, it's all perfect," I say. "I love it."

You pinch the key with your fingers, trying to distract yourself away from the tickling sensation moving up your chest and throat. You cough once and then again. The third time, a fit of coughs come out all at once. When it's over you're holding your throat and apologizing for it.

"Still happening?" I put a hand on one side of your warm face.

"It's nothing, Emmett."

I told myself the same thing and gripped the flask you gave me. The next voice I heard wasn't yours. The couch, the living room, and Christmas evaporated.

"She's gone and she's not coming back, Em. You know that, right?" Brian walked closer.

"I know."

"Were you drunk during the fight?"

"No," I almost laughed. "You're with me every second. I think you would know, bud."

"I never know with you," he laughed, "you're a sneaky fucker."

The room went quiet for a minute. I could hear muffled voices from the hall. I sat down on the bench and Brian sat next to me. He looked more and more concerned. I took another drink of gin and offered him the flask.

"No, no... If my old lady smells that on me, she'll kill me dead," he laughed again.

I looked down to the laces on my shoes, to the flask, to the line of lockers, and then down to my laces again. "I saw her out there in the crowd tonight, Brian. I saw her when I was knocked down. I saw her... and then I got back up again. It was her."

"It wasn't her, Em," he reasoned. "Maybe someone that looks like her, maybe no one at all, but not her. She ain't comin' back, Em. She isn't a part of your life anymore."

*Was he right?* I pondered. *Was there truth in what he said?* I drank again in silence.

"How long has it been?" Brian asked.

"Since I've gotten laid?"

"No, you pill, since Anna."

"A year. A year and one day."

Brian grunted, knowing that the recent anniversary of her departure made it especially hard to function not only as a boxer but as a human being.

"You have to let her go."

"I wish. I can't. I don't know how."

Brian took the flask and drank a swallow of gin. "My old lady won't smell it by the time I get home," he said.

I grinned. My childhood friend, this crazy Polak, risking his marriage for my sorry ass.

14

"You remember when Bobby got hit," he said with a pause. "Died in Europe fighting the same war that you and I fought in. When he was killed I asked God so many fucking times, 'why wasn't it *me*?' It should have been *me*. My brother had so much more to give this world than me, yet he never made it out of the mud, and I did."

"I beat myself up more than any man has ever beat me," I said.

"You think I don't know that already?"

"I beat myself up because I wish it was *me*, Brian, not her. *She* had so much more to give this world. To heal the world... The only gift God ever gave me was to hurt people."

"You're more than that, kid. We are put here for a reason. I just don't want you beating yourself to death before you find out what that reason is. And... I can't lose the only brother I have left."

A weaker man would have wept right there. Both he and I knew that my tears and his had been depleted long ago.

"Where was it that you went away with her that time?"

"The Poconos, in Pennsylvania," I responded.

"No, the other place."

I thought for a moment. It was where she and I would have been married.

"Newport?"

"Yeah, yeah," Brian nodded. "A few hours drive, right?"

"I suppose, yeah."

"Well... You don't have another fight for at least a month. Why don't you take tomorrow off? Split from town for a long weekend and clear your head. Look at the ocean and breathe some fresh air. Find yourself, maybe. Find a way to say goodbye to Anna." He patted me on the back. "What do you say? You have that fresh Model T you've been yappin' about. Take the long drive out there. It'll do ya good. Besides, Newport will probably be quiet this time of year."

"I don't know, Brian."

"You *do* know... do it."

"I'll... think about it tonight, heh?"

Brian walked to the door. "Shower and change. I'll be outside. We'll get you home." Before the door closed completely he leaned back in. "And don't drink anymore."

"All right, All right." I held up a hand. If Brian had been born as a short Italian woman I would very often confuse him for my own mother.

I took one last nip from the shiny flask and then did as Brian wanted and compelled myself to stop. I showered quickly and put on my gray suit and tie, skipping the Dapper Dan and leaving my hair barely combed. With my duffle bag over my shoulder, I left the locker room and joined Brian in the tunnel-like hallway. We were almost to the street when a trio of boys maybe ten or twelve years old, approached us. The one in the middle held out a folded newspaper in one hand and a ballpoint pen in the other. "Mr. Roane! Mr. Roane!" The boy exclaimed. "Scratch us a note, will you? Please, sir."

"Oh lord in heaven... not again." Brian turned away.

"How about I give you somethin' better, fellas? And call me Emmett."

"Yes , sir... Emmett," one of the kids replied.

I opened my bag and retrieved one of my initialed boxing gloves. I tossed it to the boys. One of them caught it and all three became electrified with joy.

16

"Remember to share it. Don't lose it; don't trade it for cigarettes."

"Yes, Mr. Emmett. Thank you, sir!" The boys began fighting over who would hold the glove. It was little things like this that molded my mouth into a smile.

"Now scram before I give you three stooges a knuckle sandwich."

They ran away laughing and disappeared down the hall.

Brian turned to me, "You know we'll have to buy more gloves again, Em."

"Just buy one glove. It's not that big of a deal."

"It doesn't work that way, Thomas Edison. They come in *pairs*."

"Speaking of Edison, thanks for dimming those fucking bulbs. Those things should be used by coppers in interrogation rooms. Jesus. I think I got a headache regardless," I said, pressing my finger to the side of my head.

"It's the thought that counts," Brian said.

It was a cool, dry night in Brooklyn. The door Brian and I exited was opposite the front entrance, enabling us to successfully circumvent the crowd. We could still hear the mass of people, though: still drunk, still elated.

"You'd think they saw a championship match," Brian cracked.

"Wait, that wasn't for a championship?" I joked. The fight wasn't a championship match at all, In fact, it really wasn't worth anything, yet it still drew a crowd.

"Get in the car, smartass," Brian said.

We entered his red 1921 Hatfield coupe convertible. The top was down and I tossed my bag in the back as the engine roared to life. We sped by a flickering street lamp, passed a bread truck at the end of the street and hooked left.

# 3.

My apartment, also in Brooklyn, wasn't far from the arena. As Brian's Hatfield glided through familiar neighborhoods, the loud engine temporarily disrupted games of stickball in the street. Dogs barked at the red car, playing the part of bulls charging a matador. Once we passed, both boys and dogs chased the convertible until it gathered speed again.

"Remember when we were those kids?" I asked my friend.

"We're still those kids," he said as he made another turn. "Part of us, anyhow."

I lived on the second floor of a two family house. The green paint was chipping and the stairs, both outside and in, felt rickety as you walked up or down them. I was careful not to bring home any woman who weighed more than or as much as I did. The combined weight of two adults walking up those goddamn stairs frightened me. Furthermore, the thought of two adults partaking in bedroom acrobatics troubled me. I was certain that eventually I would end up, on top of some doll mid-nookie, in the parlor of Mrs. O'Grady's apartment below – right when the old hag was having her tea.

Despite my very real fears regarding the dilapidated building, the debauchery went on as it did, and so did Mrs. O'Grady's broom against her ceiling. Gals and booze and nefarious nights were dandy distractions, but temporary, always temporary. I missed Anna nightly and sleeplessly. As soon as the drink and the afterglow of sex wore off, I was left with a past that invaded the present like some bat out during the daylight, lost and sick and directionless.

Brian parked in front of my place. I shook hands and thanked him for the ride and for everything else. I pulled my bag from the back and closed the car door. Before I could turn away I heard his voice again.

"Think about what I said, Em."

I looked at him and then to the night sky. "I will."

"It ain't a crime to put yourself through hell. We all do," he said. "Its just a crime to stay there."

I nodded quietly.

"So climb out of hell, Em, before I have to pull your ass out again." He smiled.

"I'll see what I can do."

"If you decide to go to Newport, leave early. Make a weekend out of it."

"What if I go and decide not to come back?" I kidded.

"I hope you don't come back. I hope the Emmett I *knew* comes back. The one that smiled all the time, like how you're smiling now, ya big baby."

I nodded again. He was right.

"*Go* to Newport, just call me in the morning."

"Will do."

"Goodnight, you sack of shit." He lit a cigarette between his lips.

When Brian drove off a tidal wave of exhaustion slammed into me again. *Perhaps it will be easy to sleep tonight*, I hoped. *Probably not, though.*

I made the treacherous ascent to my apartment without my foot going through the stairs. Once inside I dropped my bag and cranked the phonograph to play Paul Whiteman's "Three O'clock in the Morning," a song that seemed to epitomize my existence over the course of the past year. The record began with the glorious ringing of bells rising above the snaps, cracks and pops of the disc. I have many records, but this is my favorite. It's a miracle it hasn't caught on fire from the amount of times I've played it.

What little was left in the flask was gone before the song was halfway through. I poured a glass from the bottle of gin before stripping everything but my undershirt from the top half of my body. Another glass of gin. Another play of "Three O'clock in the Morning." I would play it three times before I played something else. Another glass of gin. One last play. I fumbled with the other records. Another glass of gin down the hatch. Delicious.

Mrs. O'Grady started thumping her broom below me.

"I'm not even *fornicating*, you wench!" I shouted drunkenly at the floor.

The charred remains of a cigar beckoned me to a nearby ashtray. I'm pretty sure it winked at me. I sparked a match and lit the bastard on fire, immersing myself in a cloud. I opened a window for ventilation and was hit with autumn air that felt good, no, great.

Another glass of gin. Mrs. O'Grady thumped the floor. Well, in her case it was the ceiling, or was it the floor? Whatever; no matter. I sat in the chair at my desk. What a marvelous chair it was. Best piece of furniture I have ever owned. The damn thing had wheels. I rolled around my apartment. Partially because it was fun as hell, partially because I was drunk. I mostly just wanted to piss off Mrs. O'Grady even further.

What time was it? No matter. Another glass of gin... for Anna.

For Anna.

This was the part of the night I *didn't* like, the part that started off with me looking at a picture of myself in my Marine uniform hanging on the wall, and then pictures of me boxing, training, and posing. That wasn't so bad, I suppose. They were on the walls for friends and dames to admire.

Then *it* would happen. I would find the box, that blasted box, and open it. A box that I should have cast away but couldn't bring myself to do so. I even went as far as locking it and hiding the key on myself whilst splifficated, thinking that I wouldn't find it. On several occasions I ripped my apartment to pieces to find it, and find it I did, every time.

The box contained eighteen photographs of Anna and me, some of them just Anna. *She, not I,* should have been in pictures or shows. There we were, in a park or at a fair or God knows where doing God knows what, smiling, laughing. In some I was holding her, in others she held me. Her necklace was in the box, too, the key with the heart attached to it. The engagement ring would have been in there, too, but she was buried with it, as she wished. A picture of us in the Poconos. A picture of us at her parents. A picture of us in Newport, outside of that inn we stayed at. What was the name? The Homespun?

Anna... you aren't gone. You aren't gone. You aren't gone. Maybe if I said it one hundred times it would be true. One hundred and one times? One thousand? I'll *will* you back and alive. Baby? Anna...

I opened the desk drawer and stared at the .38 Smith & Wesson. There was one bullet sitting next to the cartridge box. I loaded it into one of the six vacant holes and snapped the gun closed. I rotated the cylinder so that when the trigger is pulled, the hammer will rise, the cylinder will align and the pin will fall on *that* bullet. I placed the pistol to my temple and pressed it into my scar. *I'll finish the job that fucking heinie failed to do.* The barrel felt like a cold coin against my skin. I squeezed. More. More.

Out of the corner of my eye I saw the hammer rise. *I'm coming, Anna.*

"No," you whispered. "Please."

"Let me."

"No."

"Why?"

"Save them."

"Save who?"

"Save them," you said. "Live, Emmett."

You're gone and I breathe heavily. The .38 fell from my hand and clattered on the floor. The rest was lost to me like a tugboat in the middle of the foggy Atlantic. In the middle of nowhere. I was nowhere. The world swirled and faded to nothing.

# 4.

When I woke up, sunlight was sprawled across the desk beside me. I had passed out in my rolling chair, the top half of my body folded over my desktop like a broken accordion. I heard several car horns far outside, along with the sound of children hollering. My dumb, drunk ass left the window open, the early November air was a cruel reminder that winter, my least favorite season, was coming.

I sat up at my desk, feeling hungover, cold, and worried. The phonograph was still rotating somehow, mimicking a merry-go-round deprived of riders. It scratched and popped without music, similar to my mind when I was sober. I looked at the pictures and the necklace and the box. *Had I put them away?* "I did," I answered myself out loud.

The drawer in front of my chest was open by about three inches and I could see the corner of the box. I blinked hard and shut the drawer. Sunlight bounced off the desk to create a near-blinding orange glow as I sat up further, cracking my back against the chair. My hand shot up to shield my eyes. The clock above my desk told me it was just after nine in the morning. I looked down and saw it: the .38 Smith & Wesson. Most of the gun was hidden under the desk, leaving only the back half of the grip in sight. I left it there for the time being. Finally, I stood from the desk and shut the window. I closed the record player before walking into the kitchen.

At the sink I lowered my head between the dirty dishes and drank from the faucet, pausing to splash water on my face. It's a good thing I didn't have a doll over. If anyone saw me at that sink I would have been mistaken for a wounded animal during a drought. Perhaps I was that thing anyway.

Newport. What about it?

Was I actually going to go there?

Make the however-many hours drive and try to go back in time? Find myself so that I could find a way to move on? Go backwards so that I could go forwards?

I laughed. It sounded like some automobile advertisement in the papers... the funnies. But seriously, was I gonna go through with this shit?

*Enough with the fucking questions, Emmett.*

*Just go,* I told myself. Staying in the apartment another night would be an exact repeat of last night, which was out of the question. Going out to speakeasies, gin joints, or parties around Brooklyn was played out, despite the free drinks I always got.

So... Newport. If I was going to go away, why not there? Brian was right; it wouldn't be busy. I walked around the apartment aimlessly. Where would I stay?

I'd find out when I got there.

I threw my leather suitcase on the bed and packed my things. My gray suit, my brown suit, my better shoes, Dapper Dan pomade, socks, and underwear – always a good idea. I packed bathroom accessories, minus the razor. I shaved yesterday and if I grew some fuzz, so be it. I wasn't going to be wooing any women or spreading any gams anyway. Maybe I'd leave a will and testament before I went. "Brian, if I do not return from Newport, please, for the love of Christ, give my razor to Earl 'Curly' McKlellen so he can rid himself of the pubic hair residing upon his scalp. Amen."

I replenished my flask, then tossed the gin bottle in my suitcase. *That's everything*, I thought, *everything except...* I returned to the desk and opened the main drawer again. With trepidation I picked up the box. I stood there holding it in front of me as if either *it* or *I* would crumble to ashes if I put it down again.

The soul is a strange thing: it will pull you in one direction as your mind pulls you in another. My soul wanted that box open. It wanted to crawl inside that tiny square space and hide in the darkness with what was once tangible. The lid rose an inch before I gained control of myself and silenced it. I placed the box gently in my suitcase, a decision that was dangerous, but I did it anyway. *Call Brian*, I reminded myself.

I picked up the phone and spoke to the operator. She sounded lovely and I immediately wondered what she's wearing. *Calm down, Emmett.* She connected me to Brian.

"So... you're gonna go, ya putz?"

"Yeah, yeah... I'll go," I replied.

"You packed?"

"Yeah, yeah."

"You got reservations somewhere?"

"No."

"Well, fuck it at this point anyway. You probably don't even need it this time of year."

"I figured that, yeah."

"Cross that bridge –"

"– when I get to it," I finished. He laughed.

"Remember to go to the bank and get some cash."

"Yes, mother."

I could visualize him rolling his eyes.

Brian continued, "I don't wanna hear from you or about you unless you get arrested or you die. Don't do either of those things. This is an *escape*, Emmett, so don't go calling me or any of the dames you've been screwing or screwed. Right?"

I grunted into the phone.

*"Right?"*

"Yeah! Right!"

"All right, now go. Be safe and have a swell time."

"Thanks for everything, Brian."

"You don't have to thank me."

"Fine... I'll see ya next week," I said. "Don't miss me."

"I won't." He disconnected.

I hung up the receiver and noticed the .38 poking out from under the desk. I bent down and as I picked it up its cylinder popped open. The back of the single bullet stared back at me like a friendly one-eyed entity. I snapped it closed again, leaving the round inside. The gun found its way into my luggage, another decision I knew I probably would regret. I deliberated over it while sitting on the toilet.

As I left the porch and put on my black fedora, I smiled at the thought that I would be spared Mrs. O'Grady's brooming for a weekend. I pondered if she ever used that broom to actually sweep with or if it operated strictly as an anti-fornication apparatus.

I buttoned my pea coat and shuffled over to the garage at the end of the narrow driveway. I had bought my forest green 1926 Ford Model T earlier in the year and it was undoubtedly the nicest set of wheels I've ever known. I opened the double garage doors, rolled her out and closed the garage. With my new suitcase in the back I looked through the windshield and took a deep breath. The engine caught and I high-tailed it out of the driveway.

I used what was left in my wallet to fill up the gas tank, then stopped at the bank and withdrew one hundred dollars in cash, probably too much for the weekend, but what the hell. I hit the road before eleven, skipping the Brooklyn Bridge and using the 59th Street Bridge to avoid riding through half of Manhattan.

Not long after I left the city I noticed the trees and their extravagant colors: bright red, yellow, and orange. Had I forgotten about this? I loved growing up in Brooklyn, but I hated the fact that I was gypped out of being surrounded by New England's foliage. At times I could have sworn I was driving through a golden tunnel.

The last time I traveled through Connecticut was with you, Anna. Do you remember? I can see you holding your hand out the passenger window and catching a leaf as it falls.

"I got one, Em!" you say.

"Good catch, baby." I smile from one ear to the other.

"I know I am, but what are you?" you laugh.

We laughed. So much.

I focused on the road in front of me. A leaf landed on the glass. Maybe it was *you.* Maybe you were saying hello. Before I could reach my hand out the window and grab it, it flew away.

The Model T rolled onward. I listened to the pretend radio in my mind and the wheels against the road. A soft breeze nearly whisked me to sleep as I drove past a sign for some small town called New Canaan, another for Westport, then Fairfield. I stopped in New Haven for thirty minutes or so. I tended to the Model T's water and gas levels and made sure she wasn't in the mood to quit. More importantly, my stomach needed fuel. I crammed down a late breakfast and some coffee at a diner the size of a shoebox.

The rough road welcomed me again. I lit a cigar and increased my speed, killing an hour here and an hour there. The trees became slightly less colorful and more barren; I was getting close. I passed a sign for Rhode Island. The roads were smaller and more rugged than those in Connecticut and especially New York. Houses were further apart from each other. It was quieter. I checked the map as I drove and saw that I made a wrong move. Shit.

I turned the car around, backtracked and made the correct turn. The Model T crossed over a large bridge and as it did I looked out over the vast, glistening water, mesmerized for a moment.

After spending most of the day driving I finally saw the fancy sign for Newport. I recognized it before I could even read it. I could already smell the ocean, or perhaps that was my imagination.

# 5.

Thirty-four miles from Newport the city of Providence was enveloped in fog. In a vacant alley, three men sat in a large black truck marked "Del Vecchio Dairy," although their cargo had nothing to do with milk or cheese. They were Italian, two of them first generation in the states, one born in Italy. All of them were dressed in dull clothing.

"Where the hell are they?" The driver asked, talking to himself without knowing it.

The man to his side and the man sitting behind them on a crate both looked at their pocket watches, all brooding over the same thing. It's nine minutes after four in the afternoon, which is nine minutes too many. A black cat leapt from a pile of garbage, crossed in front of the dairy truck and disappeared between some buildings.

"Bad sign," said the man in the back. He raised his cap to get a better look. "Black cat, bad cat. I don't like it."

"Shut up, Giuseppe," the driver said, with a sliver of nervousness between his teeth.

"Just saying." Giuseppe tilted his head.

"These guys are never late," the man behind the wheel said. "Maybe they got a new driver."

"Coulda stopped to take a shit," said the man next to him.

"I doubt it," said the driver. "Knowing this egg he would rather soil his trousers than be late for a pick up."

"True…"

Fog grew thicker in the alley. The inside of the dairy truck felt more like a cramped waiting room within a developing nightmare.

The front passenger turned to the driver. "How much longer you wanna wait?"

"Five minutes."

"Three," the man on the crate interjected.

The two in the front turned slightly and looked back at Giuseppe.

"Three minutes and if no truck, no deal. We leave and phone Frank."

The two men in the front nodded warily and faced forward, hoping no more black cats crossed their line of sight. The front passenger placed a cigarette between his lips and extracted a box of matches from his pocket. The first match died in his hands, the second sparked but suffered the same fate. A third match lit the cig. He cracked a window, allowing the smoke to ascend up and out, eventually mingling with the fog.

"Third time is a charm, heh amico?" The driver said.

"I tell that to ya motha every time she grabs my meatballs."

"Don't talk about her that way, ya pisser. My mother makes the best meatballs."

"I wasn't talkin' about her meatballs, I was talkin' about mine. Clean the candle wax out of ya ears."

Giuseppe leaned forward from the back and spoke again with a sudden seriousness.

"You doppio idiota ever see a cat catch a mouse?"

"Still stuck on the fuckin' cat, Giuseppe?" said the driver.

"Of course we've seen a cat-mouse charade, we all have," the smoking man said as he tapped away ash and blew smoke out his nose.

"We had this one cat in the old country," Giuseppe said in broken English. "He'd been around for a while. I forget his name now. Mean cat. Got even meaner when mio padre brought a new cat, baby cat home. New cat everyone loved. New cat ate most of the food, ate most of the love. Take, take, take. I remember that old cat began killing more and more mice. I think to myself... *Maybe he kill cause he mad. Maybe cause he hungry, starving. Maybe he not loved and he's a bored animal.* I watch him kill fifty mice, hundred mice, maybe more, never quickly. He would torture for what seem like forever before he killed mouse. I never understand that damn cat."

The three men were silent for a moment; only the end of the cigarette crackling upon inhalation could be heard inside the truck's cab.

"Well, Giuseppe, most of the time we can't understand you. So that makes it all even, don't it?" The driver said. He and the front passenger laughed.

"Cycle of life," the smoking man said.

"Cycle of life," Giuseppe repeated.

Just then headlights could be seen coming down the alley. The beams shined through the back windows of the dairy truck and glared off the rearview mirror. The trio went quiet as a 1924 salmon-colored Studebaker Big Six sedan groaned past them and pulled to a slow stop in front of them on the opposite side of the alley.

"Well, I'll be a monkey's uncle," the driver said. "Better late than never."

"Wait," said the man with the cigarette. "That ain't what they usually show up in."

"It's probably like I says before, they probably got a new driver… hence the new wagon. That's all."

"I don't know…" said the passenger skeptically.

Giuseppe pointed to the dashboard. "Flash 'em the lights."

The driver flashed the headlights twice.

"Again," said Giuseppe.

The driver flashed the headlights once more. In the back of the salmon-colored car, someone held up a large flashlight and turned it on and off three times, returning the signal.

"Three and three, good enough for me," the driver rhymed. "It may not be the usual truck but it certainly looks big enough to handle the load."

"It looks bigger than other Studebakers I've seen," said the passenger as he stabbed out his cigarette. "It looks… *armored*."

The hardtop Studebaker across from them was indeed odd looking. Its tires were heavy, with extra deep treads. The sides of the car looked as though extra metal plates were riveted onto the exterior. The glass was thicker and difficult to see through. What was most unusual about the windows were the circles cut into them the size of silver dollars.

The driver of the dairy truck looked at the man to his right.

"You got another smoke?"

The passenger said nothing and handed him a cigarette.

Without warning, two men stepped out of the back seat of the strange armored car, from opposite sides of the vehicle. They both held something heavy.

The dairy truck driver pinched the cigarette between his lips and leaned towards the man beside him. "Light me up," he said. The passenger struck a match, this time igniting one on the first try.

Bullets tore into the dairy truck like dozens of angry hornets. The inside of the cab became a tornado of broken metal, glass, and fabric. Rounds of .45 caliber and .30-06 ripped into the bodies of the men in front, striking every square foot their lives occupied. Several shots made their way through the seats and knocked Giuseppe off his crate and onto the floor of the truck, leaving him gravely wounded. He heard the deafening whistles and impacts inside the truck and the gunshots outside, their rapid booms amplified by the buildings.

Two men stood in fog mixed with haze created by their automatic weapons. The shorter of the two, dressed in a long coat, held a Thompson submachine gun with a drum magazine. The larger of the two, and he was much larger, lowered a Browning Automatic Rifle, the barrel hotter than a radiator pipe. A third man exited the driver's side of the armored Studebaker. The men holding the now empty machine guns handed them off to the third individual, then pulled pistols from the folds of their clothing. The small man cocked the slide of a Colt 1911. Holding a humorously petite revolver in one hand, the big man removed his bowler hat to clear sweat from his brow, briefly exposing his bald head.

A fourth man stepped out of the front passenger door, his thin, wiry shape almost obscured by the veils of murkiness around him. His voice sounded as though it came out of a radio or phonograph, every word cracking crisply. He turned to the wormy man holding the heavy firearms.

"Wallace, put the cannons back in the Kettle, please. They have served their purpose for today."

Wallace returned the B.A.R. and Tommy gun to the back seat.

In the cargo bed of the dairy truck Giuseppe lay bleeding profusely and prayed that the men would drive away. *Who the hell calls their car a Kettle?*

"Owen, Nicky, you know what to do." The wiry leader nodded his men forward.

Owen, with the bowler hat, was the larger of the two. Nicky, the shorter one, sported a long coat that covered his round body, his large-brim fedora topping his wide face. His too-long sleeves almost touched the rear sight of the 1911 gripped in the sausage fingers of his right hand. The two men advanced, pistols pointed at the truck. As they neared the running board of the driver's side, Owen motioned for Nicky to go around to the passenger door. Nicky nodded and moved to the other side. They peered in and saw that the two men in the dairy truck were beyond annihilated. Expressionless, Owen signaled to Nicky and then back to his boss, indicating the job was done.

"The back… open it up now, Owen," said the boss from a distance.

"Sir," the big man acknowledged.

Owen moved guardedly down the length of the dairy truck while Nicky did the same on the other side. Once at the rear, Owen grabbed the handle of the left door as Nicky grasped the right. On the quiet count of three, both men flung the doors open, pistols aimed inward.

Unlike his bullet-riddled counterparts in the front seat, Giuseppe didn't have a pistol in his jacket, which probably contributed to him pissing his pants. When the doors swung open, he raised his hands to surrender. Lying between the wooden crates of whiskey bottles, the Italian waited for a sharp crack to end his existence.

"One a dem is alive back here, sir!" Nicky shouted.

"Better take a look at this," Owen's deep voice carried in the alley.

"Very well," the slim boss said near the Studebaker.

Owen looked back into the truck at Giuseppe. "Don't move a fuckin' hair, prick."

Giuseppe lay still, hoping that he would bleed out before whatever might happen next.

The boss turned to Wallace. "My pistol, please."

Wallace fetched a Mauser C96 from under the back seat and handed it to his boss, along with a strip of 9mm rounds. The boss loaded the handgun and cocked it adamantly. He walked to the back of the dairy truck at a slow and casual pace, the Mauser dangling from his hand.

The man twitched as he walked, as if some unseen force pinched at his organs, sparring to get out. He reached the open back doors of the truck and gazed inside. The pupils of his eyes, blacker than those of most men, were the size of pencil tips.

"Get the rodent out, gentlemen."

Owen and Nicky holstered their weapons and leaned into the back of the truck, pushing crates of booze aside. The big guy pulled one crate so hard that it tumbled out and crashed on the pavement, breaking several bottles in the fall.

"Easy now, Owen," said the boss. "This is still precious merchandise as far as I'm concerned."

"Sorry, sir." The two mobsters dropped Giuseppe's bloody body next to the broken crate.

He screamed in pain and clutched the wound on his chest. "Just kill me, bastardo."

"Bastardo, heh?" said the boss. "I've been called worse before." He knelt down and removed a broken piece of wood from the crate.

He found an intact whiskey bottle in the debris and handed it to Owen. The giant unscrewed it and gave the bottle back to the wiry leader. Owen and Nicky then took a bottle for themselves and drank.

The boss sipped and smiled. "Marvelous taste."

Giuseppe could see, through the blurred vision of a dying man, that something was wrong with the slender man's mouth. *A scar? A birth defect?*

"Too bad you wops won't be reaping the benefits of it, not this truck at least. Only reaping that's gonna be going on around here is by me. Do you know why?"

"Bastardo..."

"You said that already. Now be polite. I'm *trying* to have a conversation here. You should *try* to participate. Last conversation you'll ever have. As I was saying..." The boss took another swig of whiskey and shot Giuseppe in the knee with the Mauser.

Giuseppe cried in pure agony. "Bastardo!"

"Bastardo!" The scarred figure mocked. "Very good! Very good! And *yes,* I am. I'm reaping all the benefits of it, too. I reaped a lot more in the past, beautiful past, before you and your fucking dago boss – Frank *Norelli* – came and mucked it all up! Took my men, most of them, anyhow. Took my women. Norelli and you fucking grease balls took it *all!* " He shot Giuseppe in the other knee.

Giuseppe screamed and cursed in Italian. The cursing became praying, none of which the gangsters could understand.

"Shut up!" The boss barked and drank some more. Giuseppe sobbed.

"Isn't that just like a dog," he said before pouring whiskey on

Giuseppe's open knees.

The wounded man went silent, his mouth and eyes open to the sky, begging to be taken from the earth. The skeleton knelt down again, the barrel of the Mauser touching the pavement, creating a tripod effect. His face was only a foot or so away from Giuseppe's now. Giuseppe could clearly see the man's disfigured features.

The fiend before him wore a charcoal three-piece suit with white pinstripes. His shoes shined almost enough for Giuseppe to be able to see his own reflection for a final time. The boss's skin was chalky white with a bluish tint around the fingernails and lips. His lips were mangled. The lower left corner of his mouth was missing; a small triangular opening exposed two or three of his teeth in the bottom row, giving the mobster half of a permanent frown. He looked as though he wasn't breathing, his body eerily still as sweat perched on his receding hairline. An aroma of opium oozed from his pores. His dark wispy hair and black eyes reflected what was inside of him like a perverse projector.

"I'm going to reap, reap, reap it all back to the way it was… and send you all to hell in a handbasket." The ghoul twitched.

"What are you?" Giuseppe asked in a faltering breath.

"I'm Luther Irvin and I'm the grim goddamn reaper for today, tomorrow, and every day until Frank Norelli and his entire family are obliterated." Luther's words sent a chill through both the Italian and his own men. He stood and pointed the Mauser at Giuseppe's head. "Sorry… I'm not sorry." The gun went off.

His men drank nervously in front of him. The thought entered their minds just as it had in the past; their boss may in truth be the devil himself. The devil in a charcoal, pinstriped suit and immaculate shoes.

"Leave the bodies where they are," said Luther. "Load as many crates as you can into the Kettle."

"Yes, boss," said Nicky.

Wallace, the gang's spectacled bookkeeper and tactician, hurried over to help transport the whiskey from the shot-up dairy truck to the Studebaker.

"Let's make it snappy," said Luther.

"Should we check the cab for guns, Mr. Irvin?" asked Nicky.

"No," said the scarred man. "We have enough of those. Just get the bottles and let's get to Newport. The rest of our party is likely already at the hotel by now."

"Very well, sir."

The last of the boxes were squeezed into the gangster's car. The four men piled inside. Fog still floated between the buildings and streets beyond. The Kettle rumbled to life and vanished from the alley, fueled by nightmares more than anything else.

# 6.

Newport was just as I remembered it, only colder. When I
visited there with Anna it must have been earlier in the autumn.
Or maybe it just seemed colder now because I was driving in
alone. The smell of the ocean brought back snippets of memories
that came and went like the signs and fence posts I passed on the
stretch of road. The salt in the air woke me up from my driving
daze and put me into a half-remembered dream.

*This place is so elegant, Anna. How fitting that you
introduced it to me.*

Closer to town, I noticed the many small neighborhoods lined
with historical homes. The larger, taller structures downtown
conveyed wealth the same way that the cottage homes conveyed
the passage of time. My Model T passed by only a few other
motorists and pedestrians along the streets. This was a place for
summer escapism and hoopla for the moneyed, and this
weekend, a chilly retreat for a battered Brooklyn boxer.

I rolled by shops that I had either gone inside with Anna or
patiently waited outside of as she explored whatever trinkets,
hats, or dresses that caught her eye. There was a café and more
than one restaurant where you could sneak an actual drink. Over
the lower roofs I could see ship masts and flags fluttering in the
November wind. I took another turn and recognized one of the
many docks that rambled out over the water. A wide gap
between two stores allowed me to catch a glimpse of the same

boardwalk I strolled down hand in hand with her. If my time with Anna was an iceberg, Newport was the tip. I felt my mind scrape alongside it and wondered if I would suffer the same fate as the R.M.S. Titanic by the end of the weekend.

A part of me had agreed with Brian when he said that exposure to the past would provide a way over it, but my faith in that method wavered as I drove closer to the ocean. *Where was I driving to anyhow?* I traversed the winding roads until I reached a long, straight avenue, Bellevue Avenue. My foot lifted from the gas and the Ford slowed down enough for me to realize where my subconscious was taking me.

There was a quaint brick inn on Bellevue Ave that contrasted the abundance of Gilded Age mansions surrounding it. The Homespun Inn was a slim building, two stories high and tucked back away from the water. I saw the sign in front of the Homespun swinging in the wind, waving to me. My foot pressed down on the brake pedal and the car stopped in front of the small lodge. I stayed there with Anna last time.

*I'll stay here,* I suggested. *No, no… that would be too much. Too many memories.*

I could have turned back and found someplace to stay in town, but I didn't; I kept going. I kept looking for *it*. The Hermann Hotel. It was no more than a quarter of a mile further up Bellevue. The Herm would be double the price for a stay, maybe triple, but worth a look. I didn't see it for the longest time. I feared for a moment that it was gone, knocked down or burned to ashes. Here one day and toppled into the ocean the next. Then, like a pearly mirage, there it was. The Hermann Hotel had been too pricey for Anna and I to afford at the time, but we did walk through it together.

It was approaching seven o'clock when I arrived there. I had been steering and shifting for hours, one more mile and my limbs would have fallen off. The sight of the place was breathtaking. I remembered the architecture of the mansion being modeled after the Grand Trianon Palace of Versailles, however smaller and cut down to a basic "H" shape. There was a constant scheme in The Hermann of glazed arched windows and enormous ionic pilasters. The theme of the Grand Trianon continued on the second story and featured a balustraded roofline that distorted a somewhat hidden third floor. The Hermann's brick construction was covered entirely in white terracotta tiles.

The sun was disappearing quickly and I feared it was too late to make a reservation. Still, I turned into the pebbled driveway. As my Model T curved around the cream-colored loop I noticed a peculiar-looking car blocking the drive. I stopped abruptly and parked behind it. The vehicle appeared to be a modified Studebaker of some sort. It was salmon in color with thicker tires, thicker paneling, and thicker glass. *Were those gun ports? What an ugly piece of shit.* I wondered who the flaming asshole was that drove it around.

I climbed out of the Ford and raised the high collar of my pea coat to ward off the brisk breeze. I would leave my suitcase in the car until I was certain I'd secured a room. Once I crossed the front of my car I noticed a valet walking hurriedly to the driver's side of the Studebaker.

"Hey kid, I hope whoever owns that thing isn't as unsightly," I said with a friendly smile.

The valet looked at me as if I read his mind, his eyes widened and his nostrils flared. "Yes, sir... I mean... No, sir. Have a pleasant stay." He entered the Studebaker and drove it down the driveway.

At that moment I suppose everything caught up with me. It was hard to believe that just hours before I was still in Brooklyn, and even harder to believe that just last night coming to Newport was simply an idea and nothing more. I was here now, at the Hermann Hotel no less, standing on the steps between a pair of lion statues. I looked across the driveway at the fountain on the front lawn and the bronze angel on top of it. The water was surrounded by a circular hedge and a round path that led further out into the yard. Preceding the entrance was another, smaller fountain, potted plants, and a configuration of low, manicured hedges. I turned and faced the glass front door, identical to the four windows, two on either side of it. Four trees stood between the five glass archways, all shaped into cones and kept in such a way that they matched the hedges to perfection. Touching the trees were four sets of pillars in pairs of two, which extended high to support a generous overhang. Above the pillars four statues perched depicting cherubs in various poses.

I entered the Hermann. Ahead a voluminous staircase curved downward from two sides before merging into one, covered by a velvety red rug that flowed down like a crimson waterfall. The rug continued the way a river does, splitting at the bottom of the stairs before it hooked around pillars and flowed beneath ornate molding that looked as though Michelangelo himself had a hand in crafting it. To the left of the staircase was a tiny store selling snacks and smokes, and to the right was the check-in desk. I walked towards the alcove, passing a couple of swanky guests.

The clerk at the desk was leaning back in his chair reading what appeared to be a thin western dime novel titled *Crywood*. I'd never heard of it. His face was buried in it as I approached.

"'Scuse me," I said.

He threw down the book and sat up so straight you would have thought an electrical cord buzzed up his ass.

"Well, *hello,* sir. *Welcome* to the Hermann hotel. How may I help you this afternoon? Or evening? Which is it…?" A puzzled look spread across his face.

"I believe we are into the evening now," I surmised.

"Yes! Yes, indeed!" He pointed into the air. "How may I be of service this evening?"

The clerk was so enthusiastic I worried his thin mustache would fly from his face and stick to my forehead.

"I understand it's a bit on the late side," I said, "but I was wondering if I could get a room for the weekend. For tonight and tomorrow night."

"Are you new to the Hermann Hotel?"

"Mostly, yes. I've been here, not stayed here."

"Well, you are in for a treat." The clerk became even more elated. I could tell that whatever it was that he was about to share with me, he had been waiting all day to do so. "Let me start off by saying that like all of the tremendous dwellings on Bellevue Ave, the Hermann has an interesting history. What makes it unique, though, is the fact that it was the only one of the homes to be transformed into a hotel. The twenty-one acre estate was built between 1898 and 1902 by a silver heiress from Nevada – the daughter of one of the four partners in the Comstock Lode. She and her husband purchased the land in 1891 and sought out the architectural firm of McKim, Mead & White to design a summer retreat suitable for entertaining parties on a grand scale. The heiress and her husband, along with countless family and friends, enjoyed the mansion for roughly twenty years before eventually selling the property and moving elsewhere in 1921. In 1923 the mansion was converted into the luxurious hotel you now stand in."

"Wow," I said.

"That's not all, rest assured."

"I'm sure it isn't."

The clerk continued, "The first floor offers a billiards room, a morning room, and a dining room separated from the rest via a marble anteroom. There is a butler's pantry with an attached service elevator that is capable of traveling to any floor in the hotel including and especially the basement."

"You don't say?"

"I do say, sir. The basement of the Hermann is used for storage like any other decent basement. What's different is the

44

tremendous subterranean kitchen and, more recently and notably… well, you'll see."

I nodded and cleared my throat. *Only if you'd let me check in, bud.*

"I will also say that the second floor contains twenty grand bedrooms of varying size, some of which have the option of being linked via doors. Every room comes with its own bath and dressing closet. Some rooms feature a queen-sized bed while others feature two twin beds. Most rooms come with a sofa, tables, chairs – "

"All very impressive and cozy, I'm sure." I halted him and pumped the brakes further with a fake laugh. "I need a room, please. Can you cure me of that, bud?"

"Very sorry, yes. Very sorry. You're staying alone?"

"Alone," I fortified with another nod.

"It is late, yes. We usually don't accept guests at this hour but I suppose I can take a look-see and see if we can squeeze you in, eh?" That's when he winked at me. I wasn't sure which was more of a rube, that clunky Studebaker that poor valet had to deal with or this clerk.

He opened his guest book and began thumbing through the pages until he came across the one he was looking for.

"Ahh," he raised his eyebrows, "looks like you're in a good position, sir. Had you arrived tomorrow you'd be *shot* out of luck. We're all booked up aside from a few rooms on the third floor. This time tomorrow they'd most surely be occupied."

The third floor, I knew it. I learned from the first time I stopped in the Herm that the third floor housed another twenty rooms that were originally intended as servant's quarters but were reinvented along with the rest of the mansion. These rooms became utilized as additional guest rooms set at a slightly cheaper price than the ones a level below. The uppermost floor of the manor-turned-hotel would likely be where I would stay. It seemed the most realistic.

"All booked up?" I asked. "Ain't this the off season?"

"Yes, sir. But this year we're hosting the Harvest Festival Ball."

"Oh, I see." *Great. More people.*

"Would you like for me to reserve a room for you, sir?"

I thought about it. *Fuck it.* "Yes, please."

"Your name?"

"Emmett Roane."

"R-O-A-N-E, sir?"

"Yes, that's correct."

I paid the man in cash and realized that staying in a cheaper room was probably a blessing in disguise. He scribbled something in the book and turned around to find a room key. Out of the corner of my left eye I could feel someone's eyes on me. I looked across the lobby and saw a tall blonde in a light colored evening gown vanish behind a pillar.

"Your room key, Mr. Roane."

I turned back to see the clerk holding out the key for me.

"Room 313," he said, "You'll find your way to the third floor via the stairway closest to us. There is also another stairway in the back of the hotel. You're more than welcome to explore after you settle in. The ballroom serves as the primary dining hall and… might I *speak* again," he cleared his throat, "about the special establishment in the lowest level of the hotel that can be accessed using the rear stairs."

"Thank you, and your name is?"

"Hames."

"Well, Hames, I'm sure I'll see you around then."

"I trust you will enjoy your stay, sir."

Before I went upstairs, I went outside to fetch my luggage, tipping the valet boy before he drove away to park my car. Back inside the Herm I began the ascension to the third floor.

I came upon the first landing, veered right where the stairs split and continued climbing. Dying emerald light rained down from above through stained glass, impersonating a traffic light, a beautiful green warning. When I reached the second floor a group of men passed me, five or six of them, most dressed well. Half of them, for some odd reason, carried musical instrument cases. They were undoubtedly gangsters; I could smell it on them. The man in the front wore a charcoal suit that matched his hair and eyes, minus the pinstripes. His face appeared powdered, like a cadaver at a wake.

His mouth...

His mouth looked like he had tried to catch a hatchet in it. Perhaps the circus was in town and his act had gone awry. The only other noteworthy goons in the pack were a bookworm and a giant. The bookworm had glasses as thick as the bottom of Coke bottles. The giant was almost a foot taller than everyone else, his steps audible over the others. He looked strikingly familiar. *Where had I encountered this tank of a man before? When?* His derby hat was pulled so low, I couldn't identify him.

The group glared at me as if I had just turned one of their sisters into a mother. They passed and I realized that in the few seconds it took for them to brush by me I had been holding my breath. I didn't know who they were, but I didn't like them.

I continued up the winding red stairs until I reached the third floor. It was already clear to me why this floor was cheaper: the hallways were tighter, the walls closer together, the ceilings lower. The wallpaper was less baroque and lacked the paintings that hung on the floors below. And yet, I didn't give two shits. I had a room in the Hermann; what more could I ask?

Room 313 was at the end of the hall in the back of the hotel. I unlocked the door and was pleased to find that it had a small window looking out onto the ocean. Other than the view the room really wasn't much more than a florid walk-in closet. I sat down on the bed next to my suitcase and removed my coat and hat. Without the pea coat on I wore only a white shirt, allowing my body to breathe. The shiny flask was still nestled inside of the coat. I slid it from the inside pocket and took a sip of gin. My body fell backwards onto the mattress and I began to slip back in time.

The last time I was in a hotel room other than for an out of town boxing match was with you, Anna. We're in the Poconos about to go to a friend's birthday party. I'm waiting in my tuxedo and I looking at my watch.

"We're gonna be late, Anna."

"I'm coming, Em. Relax."

You come out of the bathroom all dolled up and thus made it impossible to relax. You're a creature beyond comprehension. If I had the option to I would have went to heaven right then at that moment and beat you there. I stop moving, speaking, and breathing.

"I don't look too much like a flapper, do I?"

"Holy Christ Almighty…" is all I can manage. I'm sure Christ Himself would have said the same.

We cascade into each other; your brown hair falling out of the headband and over your shoulders as you laugh. The beads around your neck break and roll all over the rug. We start on the floor and make love for hours; it seems boundless. We miss the party completely. We have a party of our own.

I hold you in my arms.

48

"Marry me," you say, running your finger over my scar. "Marry me."

I woke up not in the Poconos but in the Hermann Hotel. I must have been out for maybe fifteen minutes. The size of the room didn't matter. Nothing about the room mattered. I knew I would be spending very little time in it.

# 7.

On the second floor of the Hermann, Luther Irvin and his crew of eleven men occupied three rooms, all connected by unlocked doors. Each room contained two twin beds. With a man in each bed, five of the eleven men were forced to sleep on couches, chairs, or floors. Luther, of course, slept in a bed.

The boss was awake now, though, standing in front of a painting hanging beside his bed. He studied the fishing scene depicted in it: one man surrounded by a violent storm.

"Stupid painting," he said. "This cretin doesn't stand a chance."

One of Luther's men stood behind him. He was a heavy fellow with an innocent face, who looked more like a baker than a mobster. "Maybe he's smugglin' booze into the coast, heh, Mr. Irvin?"

"Maybe you should shut the fuck up, Jay, and not defend the artist or the dunce depicted in this piece of trash." Luther turned around. "Especially because this was painted *before* the Volstead act."

"Sorry, Mr. Irvin."

"You're forgiven, Jay... Just do me a kindness and grab me some tea with a pinch of absinthe."

"Yes, sir," said Jay before walking away.

Four of Luther's men were napping throughout the three rooms, desperately trying to sleep off hangovers before another night began. A fifth man sat in the bathroom with the door open, defecating shamelessly while reading a newspaper. At a table near a window Owen and Wallace sat across from each other playing checkers, Wallace occasionally glanced down at a book pertaining to the crew's remaining finances.

Carmelo and Alonzo Pelaratto were the only two members of Irvin's outfit that were one-hundred percent Italian. They were a pair of shoot-first-ask-questions-later brothers who were originally attached to the Norelli crime family but had been ejected five months prior for reckless behavior. In spite of his hatred for Italians, Luther hired the Pelaratto brothers as additional muscle; he was desperate. Both brothers sat on the edge of one bed, obsessively cleaning the gang's arsenal and jabbering to one another in their native tongue.

Although Luther's syndicate had been whittled down to just eleven men aside from himself, his ordinance remained considerable. Concealed inside a guitar case were two Thompson submachine guns, and drum and stick magazines to go with them. The Browning Automatic Rifle and its respective ammunition were transported inside a cello case, along with a Winchester 1897 shotgun and a rare Mexican Mondragon rifle. A collection of handguns, brass knuckles and knives were thrown into a tuba case. A violin case held additional ammunition, as well as Luther's personal Mauser C96 in a separate compartment. A fifth case, originally intended to hold a wind instrument, was now used to carry something else entirely, not a weapon. While moving from place to place, Luther Irvin and his men appeared to be nothing more than a traveling band.

Other than Wallace, who was only a scratch taller, Nicky at 5' 4" was the shortest of the ensemble. With his coat removed, his plump frame was revealed. He lay on one of the sofas, resembling a rotten pear in a bucket. His hat covered his eyes as he smoked a cigarette, flicking ash every few seconds onto the floor.

Luther paced the room, twitching at the end of every stretch of carpet. The index finger of his left hand ran over the scar on his mouth.

"Gonna wear a hole in the rug there, boss." Nicky spoke like a real wise guy.

"Not as likely as you are, dropping ash onto the carpet, numbskull," said Luther.

Nicky slid a rocks glass closer to him and tapped his cig on the edge.

"Hows come we got a dozen guys cramped into three rooms like fuckin' sardines?" Nicky chuckled. "That fruity guy at the check-in probably thought we was a stack of three dollar bills."

"The only three dollar bill here is you, you squat knob jocky," Luther snapped. "And watch how you speak to me."

"Alls I'm sayin' is if I became flatulent later, yuz are gonna know about it."

"Shut your ass, Nicky. *Might* I inform you that the reason we are packed in here like canned fish is because we are running low on dough? A problem that is hopefully to be resolved after the efforts of this weekend. Additionally, you fuck, having us in *less* rooms draws *less* attention."

"If we wanted less attention maybe we should have stayed elsewheres. Someplace where the Harvest *fucking* Festival Ball *wasn't* happening," Nicky said.

Luther looked at Owen and chimed the giant's name. The massive man rose from his game of checkers, walked over to Nicky, and smacked him with an open hand so hard that both the hat and the cigarette were knocked from his cranium.

"Christ, Owen, you ass!" Nicky sat up and patted out the ashes on his chest.

"Thank you, Owen," Luther said.

"Welcome," Owen replied and returned to his game.

"We need to be frugal, Nick," Wallace said in monotone without lifting his eyes from the checkers game, "at least until Norelli is disabled."

Luther paused on the rug and turned to Nicky again. "Why don't you do something productive and fetch me the Clarinet."

Nicky stood and moseyed over to the bed of instrument cases in the other room. He rudely reached between the Pelaratto brothers and picked up the only case that wasn't opened.

The boss sat down in a chair and leaned over the coffee table in front of him as Nicky set down the clarinet case. The "Clarinet" Luther referred to wasn't for making music – well, not the type of music that would come to most minds. He carefully removed the three pieces of the opium pipe from the velvet interior using only his bluish fingertips. Luther clicked the pieces together like a soldier reassembling his infantry rifle. When it was all in place, he packed the pipe with the drug and admired it.

Luther relaxed on the lavish cushion until he was almost horizontal and lit the long pipe with a wooden match. He respired the opium into himself, a percentage of it escaping through the triangular scar on his lower lip. The smoke leaked from the upside down arrowhead on his face and floated around the room similar to a resurrected spirit. Luther's features went flat as he floated into euphoria.

"Ain't it a sinch," he mumbled. "Ain't it… a sinch."

As Luther drifted up to the ceiling he was reminded of what it felt like to actually be a boss, a man of importance beyond a space of only ten other men.

"Sir," Owen spoke, "not to interrupt your moment, but, uhh, when do you want me to round up the troops for chow downstairs?"

"Soon... Owen... not now... but soon... dear boy."

"Very well, Mr. Irvin."

Jay, the art connoisseur, reentered the room with Luther's tea. His thick hands planted the tiny cup and saucer beside the clarinet case. Jay poured a shot glass worth of absinthe into the cup and stirred it with a spoon. "Your tea, Sir."

"Thank you... you may... go now."

For some reason, likely due to the fact that his boss was as high as a fucking zeppelin, Jay pictured this as the opportune time to mention something. He was on the verge of leaving the room when he turned back around. He clutched his hat nervously in front of him, revolving the brim in his hands.

"Mr. Irvin?"

"Yes... Jay?" Luther raised his brow.

"Somthin' been... on my mind. As of the late."

"Go on... boy."

"I been thinkin' about what we aim to do Sunday and... and..."

"...And *what?*"

"...And I don't know... Sir."

"What... don't you know... Jay?"

"I... I don't know if it's... *right*. Maybe we should think about this a bit more, Mr. Irvin."

"I've done enough thinking for all of us... Jay."

All eyes in the room focused on Jay, Luther's broken lip, and back to Jay. The Pelaratto brothers stopped chatting and cleaning. Another man who had been napping peacefully opened his eyes and lifted the front of his hat off his face.

Luther pressed, "Don't you think so, Jay?"

"A lot of innocent people are gonna die, boss. In a bad way."

"Can I tell you a secret... before you get completely balled up?"

"Sir...?" Jay looked at the floor.

Everyone stared at Luther, none of them blinking.

"Look at me, Jay."

"Sir," Jay raised his head.

Luther leaned forward and set the pipe down on the table. Almost half a minute passed with everyone paralyzed by silence. Finally, Luther plucked the teacup from its saucer and spoke, his eyes two pebbles blackened by hell.

"No one is innocent... you lose that when you're born."

Jay looked back down to the rug and nodded. Luther sipped the absinthe laced drink and watched Jay turn around and walk away like a lost lamb.

"Oh... and Jay," said Luther Irvin.

Jay faced his boss once more.

"Tea's cold."

# 8.

It was getting close to eight o'clock when I changed into my three-piece brown suit. While fastening the buttons on the vest I looked out of the oval window and onto the gently illuminated back lawn of the Hermann Hotel. I imagined the lawn in warmer months and how on a night like tonight, it would likely be blanketed with people in their glad rags. Tonight only a half a dozen guests stood near the fountain, including a woman in a fur coat and a man wearing a heavy jacket and scarf.

*Good Lord,* I thought. *It's really not that cold out, folks.*

I was about to turn away from the window when I noticed someone else on the lawn, someone out of place. There was a slender woman standing alone, facing the ocean with her back to the hotel. Her hair was blonde and cut short in a bob.

*Could this be the woman I caught a glimpse of in the lobby?*

Not only was her off-white evening gown a little fancy for an ordinary Friday night, but it was all she wore aside from a glistening hair pin in the shape of a flower and a string of pearls around her neck. She stood with her arms and shoulders exposed, the November chill seemingly having no effect on her delicate skin. She looked like a woman waiting for something or someone. *Aren't we all?* I pondered.

She turned suddenly and walked back into the hotel, moving up the patio stairs and under the canopy before I could see her face clearly. I finally moved away from the window and donned my brown jacket. I adjusted my tie in the mirror and took a hit from my flask prior to returning it to the inside pocket of my suit, its weight comforting against my chest. Clenched between my teeth was an unlit cigar, most of one anyhow. I gnawed on it as I closed and locked my door. The key was kept safely in the front pocket of my pants.

The obvious destination for me was the Hermann's supposed speakeasy. I paused once I got to the first floor, noting that the ballroom was to my right and the morning room and billiards room were to my left. I walked the long loop of this floor, reacquainting myself with what the hotel had to offer and remembering Hames' rambling introduction upon my arrival. I noticed sophisticated planning of the interior and how it allowed for surprising views through aligned doorways that connected each room. Most of these rooms included monumental fireplaces with protruding mantels. The ballroom was the largest in Newport, spanning forty by eighty feet. The echoing space was laden with Louis XIV furniture, a small stage for a band, and a dumbwaiter leading to the basement. The ballroom, more than any other room in the Hermann, mirrored the articulation of the exterior.

French doors at the rear of the hotel lead to a terrace flanked by broad stairs on either side as well as the center. Beyond the patio there was the sprawling lawn that lead to the ocean, its centerpiece being a wide fountain. A rose garden sat off to one side of the structure, incapacitated now that colder months were impending.

A gin mill beneath a hotel of this much affluence was something I had never seen before. I had only heard of it in murmurs and a hint I picked up from Hames. *The basement of The Hermann is used for storage like any other decent basement, what's different is the tremendous subterranean kitchen and, more recently and notably... well, you'll see.*

I descended down the rear stairs and entered the bowels of The Herm. At the end of a short dark hallway, illuminated by a singular green light bulb, was a broad iron door with the word "storage" painted on it. It had a slot at eye-level that could only be opened from the opposite side. Below the slot was an enormous knocker and a door handle that probably served no other purpose other than to make the metal block before me look a little less like a furnace.

I wondered for a moment if this was the correct door to the speak. It certainly looked the part but the fact that I could hear no music or voices coming from the other side bothered me. *What if it actually is a storage closet?* The door's knocker was heavy in my hand as I engaged it three times, the smack of metal on metal exceptionally loud in the condensed corridor. Five seconds later the slot slid open, revealing a man's nose and eyes. I could hear music behind him. The thin mustache was a dead giveaway as to who was on the other side.

"Password," he said.

"Password?" I asked.

"Yes, sir. What's the password?"

"No one ever told me the password."

The man's eyes narrowed and the slot shut in a flash. *Was I just denied access?*

The slot slid open again and I heard him laughing on the other side. "I'm just razzin' ya, Mr. Roane! Get in here!"

Hames opened the door by about a foot and a half and I squeezed inside. The walls and the solid door behind me did a good job of soundproofing the speakeasy. Once inside it was noisy and more crowded than I anticipated. In the corner I could see a piano, its player slapping the keys. A talented saxophonist piped out melodies in perfect timing with the drummer behind him. A stout man blew into a trumpet, his cheeks rounded outward like a puffer fish. In front of the band, two couples danced with each other. The men swung the women around, doing the Charleston faultlessly.

On the other side of the room two flappers danced on a table. The men sitting below them laughed like hyenas, every so often stealing a peak upwards. Near them men gambled on a pair of slot machines, not unlike the ones that Brian and I occasionally installed in speakeasies back in New York. Smoke from cigars and cigarettes hung in the air, just as it always did in these places, stinging my eyes until I got used to it. The space was about one-third the size of the ballroom above and maybe one-quarter as sumptuous. Aside from some wood paneling, a few paintings, and some deluxe furniture, the place really wasn't much to write home about. I had been in better speakeasies; I had also been in way worse. The sixty-plus people present in The Hermann's speak on this night or any night didn't give a crap about anything other than a good time and a good cocktail, both of which were delivered.

The bartenders alternated between pouring the straight stuff and mixing beverages. They shook canisters over one shoulder and then the other as if to roll a pair of lucky dice. The nicest furnishing in the speak was the bar itself. The dark wooden semi-circle at the rear of the establishment was polished to a shine. Carvings on both edges as well as the center portrayed knights ready for battle. The wall behind the bar carried a seemingly unlimited supply of alcohol that stretched almost the full length of the twenty-five foot long bar top. Behind the bottles were mirrors and a stuffed deer head wearing a top hat.

"I thought you worked at the check-in desk," I said to Hames.

"During the day, Mr. Roane. At night I'm a doorman down here."

"Jack of all trades, heh, bud?"

"I take it you didn't expect to see me again so soon," said Hames.

"I expect the unexpected. How the hell do you manage to stay awake throughout both shifts?"

"A lot of coffee and a lot of spirits, often hand in hand, sir."

I laughed, realizing the mix of coffee and liquor explained Hames' apparent jitteriness and enthusiasm.

"Well, Mr. Roane, don't be shy now. Go ahead and enjoy. You can find the bar and perhaps a lady or two on your own."

"I'll see what I can do," I responded, patting him on the back.

I walked away from Hames and into the fray.

En route to get a drink I was intercepted by a flapper who first grabbed my ass and then my hand. She was happily drunk, her headband slipping down to the side as she laughed in elation. "Do you wanna dance…" she slurred a bit, "or do you wanna dance, handsome?" I responded by spinning her around twice. Whoever she was, her mood was infectious. There was a lot of this going around the room. The people seemed more electrified than the dim lamps and table candles scattered about. One of the flapper's friends clutched her arm and pulled her away from me. I was relieved, especially since I wasn't ossified nearly enough to hoof it effectively. "He'll be back." Her friend winked at me and took the ass-grabber away.

I continued towards the bar. The alien feeling of being in a good mood sunk into my consciousness. The counter was lined with people both sipping full drinks and straining to order new ones. I took a seat at the only empty stool and leaned forward.

I contemplated making it easier on the bartender and ordering a gin neat but instead decided to step it up a bit and order my usual *social* drink known simply as the "south side," two ounces of gin, two tablespoons of sugar, and one tablespoon of chopped and bruised mint leaves. This was all topped with a thick slice of lemon and typically served in a tall glass. I first tasted the glorious drink while partying at the 21 Club in the city. I refer to it as my social drink due to the mint, sugar, and lemon making my breath more delightful instead of tasting like an ashtray or a bucket of bathtub gin. The south side cocktail could have been a contributing factor the night I managed to sleep with two British honeys. A night before Anna.

One of the bartenders, clad in a white waiter's jacket, finally made his way over to me. "What will it be, mister?"

"Hey bud, you think you can set me up with a south side? You know of it?"

"Sure do. You want it tall?"

"As tall as you can make it." I took out my wallet.

While the barkeep mixed my drink a boy hardly a day over seventeen leaned on the counter next to me. He wasn't dressed quite as nicely as the rest of the crowd and looked more like a paperboy than anything else. In a way he reminded me of myself in a previous life. I figured he was likely the son or kid brother of someone staying at The Hermann or a relative of someone that worked there. The other bartender asked him what he wanted.

"I'll have a whiskey and Coke," said the boy, his bitsy voice revealing his innocence even more than his lineless face.

"Coming right up." The bartender spun away.

The next part I could have predicted considering I can sense bullies coming from the better part of a mile away. The egg who approached had sandy blonde hair and wore a golf sweater that looked like it just crawled off of a putting green. The barkeep reappeared with my south side and I tipped him well. I gulped the minty beverage, the taste cooling the anticipation of ineludible violence. I studied the height of the trust fund baby. *Why the fuck does everyone I fight have to be taller than me?* This guy reeked of wealth he didn't earn and I hated him for it.

Without warning he came up behind the kid and socked him on the back of the head with an open hand. The boy's face almost bounced off the bar and his hat went flying over the counter. The people in the immediate vicinity stepped back without a word.

"Matty-boy," the sandy haired asshole snickered, "how many times do I have to tell you that you are not *allowed* in here. This is a place for *high* class. Are you *high* class, Matty?"

Matty was too abashed to answer. He stared at his reflection in the mirror beyond the bottles.

"Matty," the rich clown persisted, "answer me... are you *upper* class?"

"No," said the boy.

"You're not *what?*"

"I'm not upper class."

"That's right. I don't care if your daddy looks after the plumbing in this place. I don't care if you help him. I want you out of here. You're stinking up the place. Finish whatever queer drink you ordered and go before I *make* you go."

The standoff grabbed the attention of more and more people, all of them cringing at what was happening. It was apparent to me that no one shared the bully's sentiment. No one stood up to him either. I shifted on my stool just enough for him to hear me better.

"So the kid finishes his drink," I started. "But what if I buy him another drink after the one he has is done? He would have to stay and finish that one too, wouldn't he?" My eyes remained calmly forward, looking at him in the mirror.

"What?" The golfer turned.

"I said, 'what if I buy him another drink... and he *stays*?'"

"You ain't buying him anything."

"But I want to, I'm in a swell mood," I said. "Maybe I'll buy him more than one drink."

"Are you a little touched in the head?" He tapped the side of his sandy skull.

"Sure am," I responded.

The bully didn't know what to say next.

"Leave the kid alone," I shifted off the stool, took a sip of my drink and set it down.

"Are you drunk?"

"Not as drunk as you, pretty boy."

"You wanna step outside?"

"Right here is fine."

"What are *you* gonna do? Just what exactly do you *intend* to do?"

I allowed the dead air to churn in his stomach and then said, "I *intend* to cram you back up your mother's eighteenth hole faster than you can swing a nine iron."

He regarded my face long enough to realize that I was a breed he hadn't come across yet in his privileged life.

"Now listen, pal," he said, unsure of himself. "If you want to start trouble… fine. If you want to take this – "

I punched him in the nose so hard I could feel it break between my knuckles. He fell straight backwards, unconscious, with a red geyser flowing from his nostrils.

"Holy Moses," I heard a man utter behind me.

I looked around at the crowd. "Get him out of here, please."

Two men came forward and dragged the moaning troublemaker out of sight. Several more people began clapping. I had now laid out two men within forty-eight hours.

"Thank you, mister," said the teenager. "Who are you?"

"Not important, kiddo," I replied, deciding to remain incognito, if that was even possible at this point. I patted him on the shoulder, chugged what was left the south side and ordered two more, one for myself and one for him.

"I've never seen a guy get hit so hard," he said.

"Takes practice," was the only clue I could afford to give him. Someone his age would figure out who I was if anything else was surrendered. I had to remain a no name for as long as I could.

"I'm here with some friends." He pointed to a spot near the band. "You should join us. We'd love to have you."

"I'll stick by the bar, kid. Maybe another time."

"The offer stands." He shook my hand vigorously. "Thank you again, mister."

"You don't have to thank me," I said.

"I do. That guy has been a headache of mine forever. A headache for everyone."

"Well, now he has a headache of his own."

"Sure does."

The barkeep handed me the boy's cap. I tossed it to him. He caught it and held it up in his right hand gratefully before walking away. I returned to my stool, hoping the rest of my evening would be conflict-free. The bartenders conversed with each other and for a moment I thought they were about to call some muscle over to haul me out. It wouldn't have been the first time. One of the white-jacketed men walked down the bar; his smile was a relief to see.

"We decided your drinks are on the house tonight, sir."

"For what reason?" I asked.

"The reason being that you just single-handedly decommissioned the biggest son of a bitch in this entire place. You have our gratitude."

I thought about the group of instrument-toting circus goons I passed on the way up the stairs earlier and figured maybe the barkeep hadn't met everyone just yet.

"No, no, please. I can't accept that."

"We insist, sir. Drinks are on us."

I would be lying if I said I *actually* wanted to refuse the offer. Free drinks, fine. The area around the bar settled back into the rhythm it possessed before the nose breaking. To my left were three people, all waiting for a drink. When their orders arrived they dispersed, leaving a void of three stools. I looked across the blank space until my eyes met someone else's. That's when I saw her.

Not Anna, no. This was someone else entirely, someone very different, yet oddly familiar.

It was *her*, the tall blonde with the bob cut and creamy evening gown. The flower pin in her hair signaled at me through the smoke and darkness. She appeared as a sublime hybrid of both predator and prey. Her catlike eyes were almost as gold as her hair and terrifyingly magnetic. Her nose turned slightly upward as if to perpetually ask God a question. High cheekbones and a pointy chin gave her face a beautiful sharpness that could mince any suitor's best moves into yesterday's pork chops. I broke eye contact with her, unable to handle it.

I gazed forward, drinking my south side and struggling to formulate a plan. When I looked back in her direction she had moved to the stool directly to my left. I almost released an audible sound of fear. *Had she just materialized there? How did she move so swiftly? Oh Christ,* I felt the gears of my brain jam. *Oh damn me to hell. She's even more glorious up close.*

I mustered the courage to turn my head back to her. She was already staring at me again. *Jesus.* She had on dark red lipstick, pearls laced over a silver amulet around her neck, and a bracelet that slipped down her wrist as she raised her hand to cup that pretty chin. She couldn't have been older than twenty-five.

"So you gonna say somethin' to me, tough guy, or you just gonna sit there like a cheese?" Her voice was rough yet aristocratic.

"Uhhh..." was all I could manage.

"Uhhh..." she mocked me. "Not as swift with the words as you are with the punches, huh?"

"I usually am, dollface."

"Well, you aren't impressing me yet... dollface," she retorted.

"I just met you five seconds ago."

"And the clock is ticking." She finished her drink.

"What are you having?" I asked.

"Manhattan."

I flagged the bartender over and ordered her a new one.

"You really know how to impress a girl," she said.

"By getting her a drink?"

"By knocking out bad guys, you ham. That guy whose clock you cleaned was a real –"

"Jackass," I said.

66

"Yeah. Everyone had a beef with him. He tried to put a hand up my dress last night and I slapped him."

"Evidently not hard enough, madam."

"Would you like to find out?" She leaned in and smirked. "And don't call me *madam*."

I realized then that I was dealing with a bearcat. I smirked back at her and found myself lost in what to say next.

"I'm kidding," she said. "I'm Maude, Maude Mable, in case you were wondering."

"I wasn't wondering," I teased. "But thanks for sharing, Maude Mable."

She rolled her eyes at me the way someone does who has known your brand of humor for years.

"I'm Emmett." I said. "Emmett Emerson." I chuckled.

She looked at me like she just found out I had syphilis. I couldn't figure out whether I gave the bullshit name to remain incognito or to try to sound funny.

"You're not funny," she said.

"It's Roane… Emmett Roane."

"Irish," she nodded.

"Half Irish, half Italian."

"My condolences," she smiled.

The bartender came back with her Manhattan. She drank in a bewitching manner.

"So what do you do, Mr. Emmett Emerson Roane?"

"I'm a high-class male prostitute."

"I suppose I couldn't afford you."

"Exceptions can be made."

"Is that why you clapped that fella a moment ago? Gave you hell about your prices?"

"No," I said. "He tried to put his hand up my skirt."

"Touche." She clinked her glass against mine. "At least we have one thing in common."

"I'm a boxer," I said. *Why, Emmett? You fucking fool.*

"Honest?"

To my relief it appeared as though she didn't know who I was.

"Yeah, honest. Taking the weekend off." *Another stupid sentence.*

She laughed, "Taking the weekend off? You just…"

"I know… I walked into that one didn't I?"

"You're a glutton for punishment, Mr. Roane."

"So I've been told. Call me Emmett."

"Very well, Emmett. Where you from, anyway? Not around here."

"Is it that obvious?"

"Yes," she batted her eyes at me as if to fan away my ignorance.

"I'm from Brooklyn."

"Oh? An Irish-Italian boxer from Brooklyn. This is gonna be a long weekend."

"You're so sure you'll be seeing me after this drink, Maude?"

"Don't kid yourself, baby."

This dame was something else.

I looked around for a man or a friend that might come and steal her from me. I saw no such characters.

"You're here alone?" I inquired.

"I'm here without a safety net... like you. Makes things more colorful, wouldn't you agree?"

"You're not wrong."

"People with safety nets are always the least interesting," she said as if it were some devilish secret. "You have no idea what you're getting yourself into by coming here."

"Yeah?" I brushed my hand against hers, " I haven't gotten myself into anything yet, gorgeous."

"Calm down, lover-boy."

"Do I look calm to you?"

Another roll of those enigmatic eyes.

I said, "You're either from Manhattan, hence the drink, or around here. Which is it?"

"Around here, unfortunately."

"Why unfortunately?"

"A girl can get bored."

"I've only been here for a few hours but it seems like a pretty fun place to me."

"Oh, honey, you don't know the half of it," she said.

Another smile from those deep red lips. Another riddle.

"So…" I began. "Any other plans for this evening aside from flirting with boxers in bars?"

"Who said we were flirting?"

"Who said we aren't?"

She sipped her Manhattan and lit a cigarette. I popped the stubby cigar in my mouth and leaned forward for her to light it. She moved the lighter playfully at the end of the cigar from side to side. I couldn't catch the flame. I smiled with the stogie between my lips and held her hand still with my own, finally roasting the tobacco. Maude locked eyes with me and blew out the small flame.

"It's getting late and I haven't had dinner yet." She puffed. "I'll be heading upstairs to the ballroom after this drink if you would like to join me."

"I can't say I've ever had a dame ask me to dinner." I blew out cigar smoke. "Ain't it supposed to be the other way around?"

"It is, generally speaking. You're a little slow, Mr. Roane. There exists a first time for everything."

"Emmett," I corrected.

"So is that a *yes*, Emmett?"

"Yes, it's a *yes*, Maude."

"Good." Her lips curled into that mischievous smile. "Now, shut up and finish your drink, why don't ya."

*What have I gotten myself into?*

# 9.

I followed Maude to the iron door of the speakeasy. On the way there I received another pinch on my backside from the same flapper who accosted me earlier. Maude caught this and gave her a dirty look as she took my hand. We breezed past Hames, who nodded with a grin while he held the door open for us. Maude was even more intimidating as I walked behind her in the short dark hallway. Without her heels she would have been the same height as me; with them she was a notch taller. Her long legs made bustling strides towards the stairs and then up them. Her fair complexion and gray-white gown made her look like an icy tornado passing through the shadows. An urgency and voracity traveled between us. I worried that if we didn't get to the ballroom soon Maude would turn and eat me instead. Frankly, she was already eating at me in a way.

We reached the first floor and walked to our right, around a set of marble pillars. I caught up to her and extended my right arm for her to take as we approached the rear entrance to the ballroom. She hooked her arm around mine and leaned into me. "Interesting... you *are* a gentleman."

"Don't act like you wouldn't be here if I wasn't," I spoke smugly.

The host stood at the desk wearing a frilly tuxedo and the sort of smile that led me to believe he needed to use the nearest rest room – and desperately.

*Hang in there, pal,* I wanted to say, but I didn't.

His eyes flashed upon our approach. "Will it just be you and the *Mrs.* dining this evening, sir?"

I felt Maude's jolt on my arm.

I did everything in my power not to laugh out loud. *This is terrific.*

"Yes," I said. "As a matter of fact, it will be just myself and the *Mrs.* dining tonight."

"Splendid, sir. Follow me, please. This way." He picked up two menus that weighed probably as much as my car and led us into the ballroom.

"I loathe you." Maude elbowed my side.

"That's no way to speak to your husband, madam."

"I'm divorcing you."

"I simply won't allow it." I looked at her, wondering when my luck would run out. There was a simmering of something in my blood that hadn't been there in a while.

Maude and I trailed behind the host, weaving between half a dozen large, round tables until we came to a smaller one meant for a couple. Our shoes patted over the glossy wood floor, the surface so clean that when looking down I could almost see my reflection. I probably could have seen up Maude's gown, but I refrained. I was playing the role of a gentlemen husband, after all.

The expansive room was filled with conversation, laughter, and the clinking of glasses and silverware. The environment was bathed in the same apricot light as the speakeasy below, although slightly brighter and more civilized. The orange glow seemed to flow towards the center of the room from all directions. A gargantuan fireplace radiated from one end while the dimmed lights on the small stage beamed from the other. Lamps protruding from the walls parodied the candles set on each table. Above us, between two mammoth chandeliers, a panoramic view of a blue sky and clouds had been painted to mimic the open courts of ancient Rome. The picture was trimmed with gold that curled around the corners like coordinated flames. If I walked into the ballroom drunk on a clear, sunny day I likely would have mistaken the painting as reality. How someone could possess such artistic talent was beyond me.

As with most of The Hermann, the ballroom was encased in detailed moldings that spread over the walls and ceiling surrounding the depiction of the sky. On the stage a lone pianist let his fingers dance over the keys, playing a Beethoven piece that was almost hypnotic. I glanced out of the floor-to-ceiling windows and into the blackness. Nothing could be seen beyond the towering apertures. The night had taken everything. It was as if the entire world existed exclusively in this space. I didn't mind.

The host pulled out our chairs one at a time, first Maude's and then mine. We sat across from each other with a cluster of low-cut roses in the center of the table, the candle's flame glowing off the red petals. Maude's lips matched the flowers and for a second I thought that somehow one petal had freed itself and levitated between us. I smiled at the surreal splendor of the moment. This ballroom, this girl, this type of dining, were all foreign to me.

"Enjoy your meal," said the host.

He marched away and was hastily replaced by a waiter who looked so similar he could have been the host's brother. *Do they stamp these guys out in a factory?* I wondered.

The waiter leaned towards Maude. "Madam, do you need time with the menu?"

"We'll need a minute, yes," she answered.

"Are you *familiar* with our selection?" The waiter asked. "We have certain specialties."

"I am familiar, thank you kindly."

The waiter departed for the time being. As his back turned to us Maude turned her menu toward me. She was showing me something.

"See this little friend here?" She pointed to a small tab made of green felt at the bottom of the center page. I examined the tab on my own menu.

"Pull this down and you'll see *another* menu," she informed. "The fun kind."

I tugged the tab and a hidden compartment slid downward, revealing a lengthy drink list.

"Anything you want, it's here," she said. "If it isn't, they can make it."

"Interesting," I replied and admired selection and its discrete abode.

The waiter came back to the table and I noticed Maude holding the menu up higher. She flicked the green tab as if to indicate something to him.

The waiter gave a nod and simply said, "Yes."

"I'll just have a glass of wine, white. No specification. Your middle-of-the-road bottle will suffice," she said with elegance.

The waiter turned to me. "And for you, sir?"

"I'll take a glass of red wine. No preference either... Middle-of-the-road as well."

"Will do."

"Thank you," I said.

"I'll return shortly," the waiter chimed and vanished.

Maude returned her focus to me. "You flick the green tab to signal you aren't some fed or copper looking for a bust. It tells the server you are safe. Don't forget to tip well."

"So you're in the *know* apparently."

"I am," she said. "I know how to have a time."

I looked at Maude with a rascally squint. "How come you didn't get mad at him when *he* called you madam?"

"Because it's his job. You were just being a brat, and you know it." Maude held up the menu and glanced at me over the top with a soft grin. "You look like someone who is out of his element."

"Do I?"

"Fortunate that you're with good company. Must make it easier."

"To be determined." I raised my menu and deflected her playful glare.

"Most men would kill to be in your shoes, Mr. Roane."

"*Emmett,*" I mumbled.

"*Emmett,*" she purred.

"I wouldn't put it past me to kill any man who tries to take my shoes from me. Tonight or any other night."

"Like that sap you socked downstairs?"

"He'll live," I speculated.

"I'm just glad you're enjoying yourself," Maude said.

Both of us spoke from behind our menus. The cover gave me time to take my eyes off her and collect my thoughts. "I'm not exactly used to such…"

"A gal?" she chirped.

"I was gonna say dinner. But yeah, that too."

"We haven't even eaten yet."

"Speaking of which, I may need some help with that."

"You need me to feed you? *Jesus.*"

"No…" I croaked. " I mean with *what* to eat. What the hell is this stuff?"

"It's mostly French," she told me. "The chef is one of France's best. He's been here for a while now."

"So what?" I said.

"So just order something with fish. You're near the ocean; the fish is always good here. You like fish, right?"

"Fish is fine."

I studied the menu, running over words and pronunciations that may as well have been from the lost city of Atlantis. For three long minutes I struggled in silence. *Why the hell didn't they print this thing in English?* My frustration had to have been apparent.

Maude kept her laughter at bay. "Find something you like?" she inquired.

"Yes, I believe so," I replied.

Out of the corner of my eye I could see him coming. *The fucking waiter.* I recognized the word *sole*. Sole was fish. *Order that,* I commanded myself. Somewhere else on the menu I stumbled across something that looked like it was probably delicious. I made a mental note of it. In the blink of an eye he was upon us with a notepad and pen. "If you folks are ready I would be more than happy to read you the chef's specials we have tonight."

"Go right ahead, please," Maude said.

He rambled on for a full minute about all the dishes, none of which I could comprehend.

"That sounds appetizing. Doesn't that sound appetizing, Emmett?" she piped.

"Sure does," I said, with the phoniest smile I had ever muscled.

Maude chose something from the list of specials. Again, I could not comprehend. She seemed to say it with perfect French pronunciation.

*Stick with the choices on the menu, Emmett. Don't get cocky.*

The waiter finished scribbling and aimed his pen at me. *Here we go.*

"And what will it be for the gentleman tonight?"

I lowered my eyes to where my finger rested on the menu.

"I'll have… the cock-illes Saint Jackies… annnd… the soul manure."

"Sir…?" He leaned forward, head tilted.

Maude held up a hand to her face. "Forgive my husband. His French isn't very good," she chuckled charmingly. "He'll order the *sole meuniere* and the *coquilles Saint Jacques,*" she quoted in perfect French.

"Yes, I'll have that," I reiterated, again with the cheesy smile.

"Good choice, sir."

"Thank you." I nodded.

The waiter closed his pad and walked away in determined steps.

Maude was staring at me, her eyes as wide as ever. "You do realize that you initially made a genital reference and ordered manure in the same sentence, right?"

"No."

"Cock-illes and soul manure...? Did someone drop you on your head recently?" she chided.

"Actually, yes, that *did* happen. Just yesterday, as a matter of fact."

She held a hand to her face again and took a sip of white wine. "You know, you can't just expect to get by in life as a brute with devilishly good looks."

"'Scuse me, madam, that is no way to speak to your husband," I gulped my red wine.

"I already told you... I'm divorcing you." Her grin pressed the dark red lipstick onto the rim of her glass.

"Liar," I whispered.

Maude and I continued to poke at each other. She roped me in further and I hung on her every word. We talked and laughed without a bump or a pause until the food arrived. Manure or not, it was fantastically appetizing.

The simmering and thawing in my veins persisted. It wasn't the feeling of gin or wine. This was something exotic and more complex, something human, organic, and cryptic. It felt frighteningly natural. While pleasure invaded my five senses, my sixth sense flared up without warning. There was something else, *someone* else in the ballroom. From across the glossed floor, lively tables, and roses I could feel negativity. I peered over my shoulder and scanned the tables behind me.

"What is it?" Maude asked, as she cut her chicken.

"Nothing," I replied and turned back to her.

But it wasn't nothing.

~

On the opposite side of the ballroom Luther Irvin sat at a table with five of his men. The other six men sat at a separate table next to his. The mobsters drank copiously as they finished their meals and laughed obnoxiously louder than the other groups nearby. Liquor was spilled while food became contaminated with cigarette ash. Much of the silverware clattered to the floor instead of onto dishes where it belonged. Had Luther Irvin been anything other than infamous, the hotel probably would have asked that he and his party leave the dining area, or furthermore, the property. Unfortunately for the harassed waiters and agitated tables nearby, Luther Irvin *was* infamous. Infamous and unpredictable.

He sat there calmly, still hovering on opium and slurping the shallow puddle of lobster bisque in front of him. Every few spoonfuls, a chunky drop of soup would be liberated through the disfigurement on his lower lip. Luther became used to this and quickly wiped away the drop before those around him grew balls big enough to remind him. He brought the last three spoonfuls of bisque to his mouth and dabbed his scar with the corner of his napkin. Luther looked around in full realization that he was a father losing control of his children. He was thankful for the opium and its kind way of dulling this discouraging reality. To his left sat Owen; to his right sat Wallace and then Nicky.

Nicky spoke with his mouth full of spaghetti. "Food ain't bad here, heh, boss? Pretty soon we'll be eating like kings every night."

"Don't speak with your mouth full, Nicky, especially not to me," Luther asserted.

"I'm just sayin' you picked a swell chow hall, Mr. Irvin."

"And *I'm* just saying *chew* your fucking food, Nicky."

Nicky sucked a noodle through his fat lips and finished his spaghetti in silence. Wallace cut the remaining slab of his ham into tiny pieces and nibbled on them like a bird. Owen Topler shoveled bloody steak into the opening below his nose, chewing it viciously before the meat could come back to life. The boss always placed Wallace and Owen on either side of him at dinner. He could, despite their odd eating habits, count on them to be more docile during a meal.

Luther felt someone's eyes on him from across the ballroom. When he looked up, he saw a bruiser of a man seated at a small table far away. The man turned back around to face a glamorous blonde before Luther could see his face. The boss had watched the couple enter the ballroom earlier. He admired the woman and swore to Christ the man on her arm looked familiar. *From where?* Luther racked his mind. *Perhaps too much opium. From where have I seen him before?*

He turned to Owen and tapped his immense forearm. "Owen. That guy over there with the blonde. You recognize him?"

"What guy?" Owen asked.

"That guy." Luther pointed with his spoon. "His back is to us."

"Huh?"

"*That* guy... See?"

Owen strained his eyes between tables and saw the man Luther was referring to.

"Can't tell much with his back to us. I'd give his dame some nookie though, I tell ya that."

"Look carefully," Luther pressured. "I *know* I know him, and I *know* you know him, I just can't place a finger on it."

The giant leaned forward, his eyes squinting. "It can't be," he muttered.

Owen *did* recognize the man. He could see the scar that tarnished the hair on the side of the boxer's head.

"That's Emmett Roane."

~

Maude and I finished our meals to satisfaction and moved on to our second glass of wine. I was telling a story that had her laughing like a schoolgirl.

"So, I sit back down in my corner of the ring with my lip swollen to the size of a snail and my buddy Brian takes one look at me –" I'm laughing myself now "– and says, 'you can't go back out there, Em. One hit and your lip is gonna burst like a firecracker all over the canvas!'"

"You're disgusting." Maude laughed on.

"So I said to Brian," I held my lip to imitate myself with a swollen lisp, "'what do ya mean *firecracker?* I'll use my lip to *absorb* any blows, right? Like a pillow.'"

"You can't be serious!"

"As serious as the eighteenth amendment."

"So did you get back out there?" she asked.

"I was about to and then Brian says, 'hang on, let me lance it.'"

"Oh gosh." She clasped the amulet around her neck. "Lance your lip?"

I held my lower lip again to mock the past. "Lance my lip."

She chuckled and moved her hand up to her mouth.

"So he stabs my lip with a pin – blood goes everywhere – and they call the fight!"

"No!" she gasped.

"So you lost?"

"So I lost. Ref claimed too much blood."

"I don't believe it."

"It happened."

"A shame." She shook her head.

"You're tellin' me. I *had* the other guy. *Had* him."

We laughed together, sopped up more wine, and eventually caught our breath.

"Do you tell that story to all the girls?" she asked.

"Only the ones I know can handle it."

"How were you so sure *I* could handle it?"

"I can just tell."

"So you're a mind-reading boxer now?"

"Just good at reading what's in front of me… or behind me."

Our waiter revisited our table. "How is everything?"

"Wonderful," said Maude.

"Yes, it is," I agreed.

The server continued, "Before I present you with the dessert menu I must inform you that Mr. Irvin has requested that you join him at his table."

I looked at Maude. Her skin had gone whiter than the tablecloth.

"Mr. Irvin?" I was lost.

"Yes, sir. Luther Irvin." He gestured to the same problematic area I had noticed before.

I spied over my shoulder once again and considered the tables of circus folk, the same dipshits I passed on the stairs when I first arrived at The Herm. Mobsters, no doubt.

"I'm not so sure I know a Mr. Irvin, or any of those men for that matter. Are you sure you have the correct table?"

"Are you Emmett Roane?" The waiter asked.

"Ya, last time I checked."

"I'm afraid I am not mistaken, Mr. Roane."

"I think the lady and I will pass. Send Mr. Irvin our regrets, will you?"

The waiter stood awkwardly mum, his face twisted into a puzzle. Finally, he said. "I wouldn't advise you decline, sir."

"Oh yeah? Why's that, Charlie?" I didn't know if his name was Charlie, but he looked like a Charlie so I said it anyway.

Maude suddenly interrupted. "Could you give us a minute?" she asked the waiter. "Don't tell Mr. Irvin we decline... just yet. Can you come back in say... five minutes?"

The server nodded at Maude. "Surely, ma'am." He was gone, albeit temporarily.

"Please tell me you're pulling my leg, Emmett."

"Well, hopefully later on, but not at the moment."

"Shut up. I'm not joking. You seriously don't know who Luther Irvin is?"

"Never heard of this Irvin shmuck, no."

"Oh, Jesus, well…" she apprehensively played with one of her earrings.

"Well, *what?*"

"He's bad. *Real* bad."

"I picked up on that part."

"How does he know you?"

"No clue. Something like this wouldn't surprise me in New York, but all the way out here… Doesn't make sense."

Maude finished her glass of wine, and not in the same jolly fashion she did earlier during dinner.

I leaned in. "So, are you gonna tell me who he is or what?"

She touched her fingers to my wrist. "Couple years ago Luther Irvin *ran* the Providence mob. He controlled all the bootlegging and flow of liquor, not only in Rhode Island, but Connecticut and even up into Mass. He had rackets, gambling, sharking – everywhere."

"So what happened?"

"The Italians happened. The Norelli crime family took over. They killed or converted Irvin's entire operation. Made Providence *their* home."

"Seems like Irvin's doin' all right based off of what I see over at those tables."

Maude nodded in the mobster's direction. "Those two tables

over there are likely a consolidation of all the men Luther Irvin has left."

"That's sad." I joked.

"Yeah, agreed," said Maude. "But it makes him *more* dangerous. He's like a cornered animal, and more violent than ever. You should hear about some of the moves he's pulled recently."

"Like...?"

"Like burning down a church that Frank Norelli's family frequented. No one was inside but a priest and two or three people that weren't even Norellis. Took forever to identify the remains."

Hearing this, I ran out of humor. This Irvin fella wasn't bad; he was evil. Whoever this creep was, he wanted to play. *So lets play, pal.*

"Well, what are we waiting for?" I said to Maude.

"I'm confused."

"Let's join him. See what the bastard wants, shall we?"

"Emmett! Did you *hear* what I just said?"

"Perfectly."

"You've drank too much."

"I'm a middleweight, not a lightweight."

"You're mad."

"No, *he* is. Which is why we go for one drink at his table. Guys like that ain't gonna stop until they get what they want. Right now he wants me. So we say hello. We aren't gonna start necking with him, not *me* at least. We just say hello."

"You are a fool."

"And you are coming with me, toots."

"Don't call me toots."

"I'm curious, anyway."

"Curious about *what,* Emmett?"

"Curious about what the hell happened to his mouth." I flagged down the waiter and he returned expeditiously.

He leaned between Maude and me. "Sir?"

"Another white wine for the lady and a red for me. No, scratch that. Make that a Manhattan for the lady and a south side for me."

"Anything else, sir?"

"Yes. Tell Mr. Luther Irvin we'll be joining him in two minutes."

# 10.

The closer Maude and I got to Luther Irvin and his goons, the more I could see what a hideous son of a bitch he truly was. I guess the part that bothered me (and probably most people) the most was the fact that it was difficult-to-impossible to tell whether he was smiling. The scar left him with half his mouth in a permanent frown. It's rare that a person's exterior so accurately exposes the ugliness they harbor within. Luther Irvin was one of those people, a rare breed that God chose to mark in order to signal to the rest of us that some miscreation had entered a human form.

When something bad happens to someone, that individual makes a choice. Consciously or subconsciously, overtly or covertly, the choice is made and is most often irreversible. That person chooses to become better from the experience or worse. This is how saints become saints and demons become demons. The separation of heaven and hell typically happens in a single moment. It was clear what choice Luther had made and evident that he brought eleven other poor souls to the circles of Hades with him. He undoubtedly intended to bring more.

We were ten steps away from joining Mr. Irvin's party when Maude squeezed my arm. "Okay," she whispered.

"Okay, what?" I asked.

"Okay, I think I'm drunk enough for this."

"Makes two of us."

"I hate a boring night, anyway." Her mischievousness had returned.

"It wouldn't have been boring either way."

"Keep telling yourself that, mister."

Maude and I traded smiles.

My focus returned to Luther's table and recognized another notorious son of a bitch. This one I knew personally: Owen Topler, a former boxer and full-time meat-headed asshole. This was going to be just peachy.

The waiter was busy pushing their chairs together to create a gap big enough for two additional seats. Our chairs were directly opposite from Luther's seat at the round table.

"Mr. Roane," the devil sang through his limp lip, "what a pleasure to meet you."

"You as well," I replied, with a lie.

His cold eyes shifted to Maude. "And who is this striking creature you brought along?"

"This is Maude Mable," I said.

"Pleasure to meet you," Maude said.

A squat wise-guy two seats to Luther's left snickered to himself and then decided to open his mouth. "Miss Maude Mable, that's a ma-ma-ma-mouthful, sweethahht. You probably know all about mouthfuls, eh, baby?"

Maude's eyes flared; her lips pursed. "Interesting manners.

You would probably know more about mouthfuls than I would, you little tub of *shit*."

The round pot held his eyebrows high and his mouth closed. He likely wasn't used to taking any belts from a female.

"Well! I can see we're off to a great start here," Luther exclaimed with stiff enthusiasm. "If you two would be kind enough to forgive and forget him. Nicky has no manners, really."

"Apparently," Maude growled.

"*Please* sit down," said Luther. Maude and I sat, both of us taking a drink before our cheeks hit the cushions.

"Hiya, Roane," Owen Topler bellowed.

"Owen," I acknowledged.

"Allow me to introduce you to the table," Luther continued. He started to his left and moved clockwise. "You know Owen. There is Leland. Johnny. Unfortunately, Nicky. Wallace. And myself. *I'm* Luther Irvin."

"Indeed," I mused. "That other table consists of your friends, as well?"

"Associates, yes," Luther lisped.

I could tell that the only guys he honestly cared about were Owen, Wallace the worm, and, in some strange way, Nicky. For all one knows Nicky gave great massages. Anything was possible with these oddballs.

"So I'm sitting here finishing my bisque," Luther commenced, "and I look across the room and I swear I recognize you from *somewhere*. I couldn't for the *life* of me figure out from where – and then Owen kindly reminded me that you were a boxer."

"Still am," I said.

"Ah, yes. I watched you fight years ago. It was really something. 'The Butcher of Brooklyn'– was that what they called you?"

"Something like that, yeah."

"Owen here was a boxer as well. Says he had a decent bout with you a while back."

"I remember," and I *did* remember.

Owen smiled at me. I didn't smile back.

Luther spoke for the giant. "Since those days Owen has moved on to other work."

"Oh, yeah? Is that so, Owen? What kind of work do you do?" I prodded and drank.

"Like… you know," Owen answered.

"No, I don't know."

"Loose ends and stuff."

"Loose ends, you say?" I lit my cigar. "Well, that makes *one* of us."

Owen gave me a dumbfounded face that resembled a grown man who just found out he was adopted. There wasn't much in the cerebral department for Owen, but that didn't stop his attitude from being a pompous one in and out of the ring.

"Sounds pretty snappy," I continued.

"It will pay off," Owen said.

"I hope so… for your sake." I switched my eyes to the worm-man on Luther's right.

"And what about you, Mr. Wallace? What have you been doing?"

"Books, papers, planning, and such," he replied, as if he was reading from a script.

"Did Mr. Irvin tell you to say that?"

"He is… my boss."

"I figured that one out, thank you."

"I'm very busy lately," the worm said with a wooden expression, pushing his spectacles back up his nose.

"Are you now? Mr. Wallace, I gotta tell ya, you remind me of this kid I went to school with. A virgin. Made one *hell* of a tax collector later in life."

Wallace cleared his throat. "Your witticisms, while meant to be irreverent, are *irrelevant* to my mood, Mr. Roane."

"Have you been saving that one for a rainy day?" I smirked.

Nicky lit a cigarette and interrupted. "You wanna talk to someone wit a slick mouth, talk to me, tough guy!" He pointed the glowing end of the cig at me.

Maude fired up her own cig with one eyebrow raised. "Slick mouth, little Nicky? Is that what all the *boys* call you?" She chuckled and sipped.

"Shut ya pretty lips, ya quiff!" Nicky demanded.

I puffed my cigar and considered the route of the conversation. "Well," I said. "Loads of chemistry here tonight."

Luther said, "I couldn't agree more, Mr. Roane. May I call you Emmett?"

"No."

"Very well, Mr. Roane. So, what is your business in Newport? At the gilded Hermann Hotel?"

"Small vacation from the madness," I answered.

"I do hope we aren't inconveniencing you with any... *madness*."

"Not yet."

Luther aimed his broken lip at Maude. "Miss Mable, what brings you to this fine establishment?"

She inhaled smoke between red lipstick and exhaled out of her nose. "Oh, you know, just looking for a little *fun*."

Owen gleamed as much as a dumbass could gleam. "A real bearcat, huh?"

"Calm down there, big boy," she said. "I'm taken. Emmett and I have been together for... how long now?" She looked at me with a grin.

"Uhhh..." was all I could produce. Again.

"Uhhh..." She mocked. "He's so in love... *we're* so in love, he can't even remember."

"Six months?" I said.

Luther nodded approvingly and sipped whatever the hell was in his glass. The liquid trickled out from his scar and down his pale chin. There was a blue ghostliness to him that I had seen in opium addicts. Luther blotted the drip quickly with a napkin. "Excuse me," he murmured. He looked up and took another drink, this time a gulp that didn't leak.

"You two do make a charismatic couple, I must admit," he said.

"Oh, yeah?" said Maude. "What makes you say that?"

He took his time, as if he was loading the next sentence into a cannon, ramming the shell down the barrel before firing. "I come under the divine impression that you two are both transcendently damaged souls," he said softly. And he *smiled*. It was like witnessing something incongruous, like an illiterate in a library or a prostitute in church.

"Am I right or wrong?" He twisted the dagger.

I pulled from the stogie, blew a smoke ring and looked at his ugly mug through it.

"It takes one to know one, Mr. Irvin."

"That it does, Mr. Roane. *Butcher* of Brooklyn."

"I didn't get that name for nothin'."

"Ohhh, I could imagine. Quite the *bad* boy you are, Mr. Roane." He whistled. "I know a little about you. I'm surprised you haven't heard of *me.*"

"I know enough," I responded.

Luther turned to his right and extended a hand past Wallace. "Nicky, do me a kindness. Pull your head out of your ass and give me a ciggy."

Nicky quickly retrieved a cigarette from a metallic case that clicked open and closed. Luther tapped the cig on the table and then sparked it alive. Smoke crept out of that damn scar. He looked like some sort of dragon awakening from a thousand-year slumber.

"Violent men fascinate me," he said. "Tell me, Mr. Roane, when was it that you first realized you were swift in conflict?"

I smoked the cigar until the memory arrived. "I was seven years old. The school courtyard. A bully two years older than me and a foot taller hovered around me like an oversized mosquito. He caused me to bleed once before I broke his two front teeth. Broke two of my fingers in the process."

"*Wonderful, yes.*" Luther said. "Must have been quite a show."

"It was over quickly."

"But you are something *else*, aren't you?"

"I would be more inclined to say that your Owen is something *else.*"

"Well… That's no secret," Luther chimed.

Owen smirked and grunted like the ape that he was.

"Can I ask you something now, Mr. Irvin?" Maude inhaled and extinguished her cig in a tiny ashtray. "When did you realize the kind of man *you* are? Was it in a schoolyard, as well?"

"It was, actually. A bully, as well, except I didn't punch him. I wasn't strong enough."

"Did you talk him to death?" Maude quipped.

Luther looked at the painted sky above us and then down to his glass before he finished it.

"I stabbed him in the ear with a pen. I was moved to a very different school after that. Realized who I was. *Reminded* of who I was later in life, too. We all are… when we run out of options."

I exchanged a glance with Maude. I could tell she wanted to leave and so did I. The tension was becoming suffocating. Nicky let out a high-pitched sneeze that broke some of the heavy air at the table and rattled silverware.

"Baptism by fire spawns the philosopher in us all, right, Mr. Irvin?"

"I would agree, Mr. Roane."

I stood from the table. "I believe it is time for Miss Mable and I to retire for the evening."

"Yes, indeed," said Maude, brushing a strand of blonde hair back into place.

94

"It has been a pleasure," I said. "Splendid meeting you all."

"The delight was entirely ours," Luther said.

"Enjoy your evening, gentlemen," Maude added.

Luther lifted his chin to me. "I would advise you to avoid any madness during your stay."

"Sometimes avoiding isn't always enough... or even possible."

"I trust I'll see you two around, then."

I pushed in my chair. "Don't miss me," I said and bit down on the cigar.

Maude took my arm and we made our way back to our table. The waiter returned with our check. I paid with a nice tip on top and we left the ballroom with our drinks.

# 11.

The main lobby was quiet in comparison. We passed a couple on a bench likely waiting for their car and a man sitting in a comfy chair catching up on events in a local newspaper. I glanced at the front page and saw photograph of a church turned to charcoal smithereens. Above the grisly image I glimpsed, *"Mobster Suspected in..."* The rest of the sentence was lost to me as Maude and I turned the corner out of the lobby and almost knocked into Hames.

"Hello, Mr. Roane, Miss Mable. I see you have found each other's company rewarding." Again, he winked.

"Yes, Hames, very much so. Your shift over at the door downstairs?"

"Oh, no, sir. Just stretching my legs."

"You have someone manning the door while you're gone?" I asked out of curiosity.

"Oh! No, I don't. I should probably go back."

"Probably," Maude giggled.

"Oh, Lord." He rubbed his thin mustache.

"Hames, can you do me a favor and hold onto this?" I handed him my empty glass. He took it and smiled as if I had given a Christmas present.

"Yes, sir! Good night, now." He sped off in the opposite direction of the speakeasy.

"Hames! Other way!" I shouted.

"Right!" He turned around and broke into a run past us.

Maude laughed. "I think I needed something like that after the dinner we just had."

"The dinner was fine," I said. "It was afterwards that got a little dicey."

"Which was *your* idea, not mine." She bumped me.

"It was entertaining," I said, "and a bit revealing."

"And a bit unnerving," she added.

Maude was right. Then again, so was I.

"Something tells me this isn't going to be a normal weekend," she said.

"I'm not sure I would know a normal weekend if it jumped up and bit me in the ass."

Her sharp elbow pressed into my ribs again. "That's really no way to speak in front of your wife, you know." That smile of hers. Jesus Christ. What a delicacy. It was especially vibrant after looking at Luther Irvin's frown for ten minutes.

"Ohh, so *now* you're my wife?" I chuckled.

"And ... perhaps this is our honeymoon." She held out a hand matter-of-factly.

"We're off to a great start, darlin'."

"I have a wild imagination," Maude said.

I wondered if her imagination could vanquish my memories, smother my nightmares, cure me once and for all. I wondered if I was curable.

"Into the billiards room," she commanded, as if she was in *fact* my wife. Into the billiards room we went, that torrent of beauty pulling me along.

It was like entering some ancient war room of Alexander the Great. The floor was a green marble that extended up slender pillars. The room was encased in walls of dark mahogany, topped by yet another ceiling of exquisite molding. Small statues of heroes and heroines from long ago guarded the four corners of the room. There was a globe, one of the ones that if you ran your hand over it you could feel the mountains and deserts beneath your fingertips. Plush furniture sat in front of another fireplace. *How many fireplaces did this damn building have?* It was easy to get distracted upon entering any of the rooms in The Hermann Hotel.

Two dapper gentlemen were mid-game when Maude and I walked in. One man chalked the tip of his pool cue while his opponent popped the white ball into the other numbered spheres. Their girlfriends or wives chatted with one another, cocktails in hand, in the corner opposite Maude and me. I could tell by a glimpse that they were looking at us. We stood by the rack of pool cues. Maude leaned into me as I expected she would, her nose brushing my scar.

"I would venture to say that they are probably wondering to each other," she hinted.

"Wondering about what?" I faced her.

"Wondering how a feral being such as yourself wound up with the likes of me," she said with a smile and a flash of her teeth.

"So I'm feral now?"

"I'm razzing you, Emmett."

"You think you're funny."

"More funny than you." Her long finger poked my chest.

A wave of heat came over me. "Don't tease." I tried to sound tough but fell short.

"So," she sipped and leaned against the nearest pillar. "You met Luther Irvin. Most people don't have the unfortunate pleasure. *Now* do you understand what I was saying about him before we walked over to that table?"

"There is something seriously wrong with that man."

"That's an understatement if I've ever heard one."

"He's not here for shits and giggles, Maude. A man like that – in the position that he's in... the circumstances he's dealing with – he's here for a *reason*. And I don't like it at all." I looked at her.

"Tell me about the behemoth sitting next to him."

"Who? Owen Topler?"

"Yes, the bald man."

I scratched my chin and already felt stubble. I said, " He was a boxer."

"*Was*?"

"Yeah. An arrogant one. And a dirty fighter. He would throw below the belt, kick an opponent when he was on the canvas, spit on him, spit into the crowd when they hollered at him – which was often. He was thrown out of almost as many boxing rings as he walked into. The man was a heavyweight who finagled his way into lower weight classes to gain an unfair advantage. " I smoked the stump of my cigar.

"And you fought him?"

"I did, a couple of years ago. They called it a stalemate – after fourteen rounds – which never happens. I never got another crack at him, even though I tried like hell to arrange a fight. Funniest thing about Owen is that he would never block punches; he would just let you hit him and he'd keep comin'. Shots would just bounce off of him. I guess that's why they called him 'The Tank.' A real slug-proof, two-ton baby. He took what was thrown at him and absorbed it into that thick head of his. Probably explains the shortage of brainpower. He must have finally pissed off one too many people and migrated out here to do whatever the hell he does now for Irvin."

"You've never seen those other guys?" Maude drank.

"Nahh, I didn't get a good enough look at the other table. I thought maybe I knew that Wallace bookworm or that stuffed mushroom who talked sass, but no. Just another stiff and another wise guy."

"Speaking of wise guys," Maude said, "do you believe that little lump? *Nicky*, was it?"

"Yeah, I think so."

"Christ, I'd like to back my car right over him."

"Easy, doll. Maybe you'll have the chance to."

A bearcat she was. Owen got one thing right in his life.

"Enough about the dunce club, gorgeous." I put my hand around her waist. I was feeling nice and warm. "Hows about just you and me?"

"Hows about it?" she said an inch from my face.

"Is this night supposed to end?"

"It will soon enough, handsome."

100

"Down here or upstairs?"

She rolled those cursed cat eyes in response.

"A night cap in my room?" I offered.

Her smile reminded me that the rest of the weekend was in front of us. Maude downed what remained of her Manhattan and put the glass on a table close by. She walked back to me seductively, slid a hand up my neck and pressed her lips into my jawline. "I'll cap my own night."

A kiss: brief but enough to leave a mark.

"Dream of me," she said.

I couldn't tell whether it was a request or an order. It didn't matter. I wanted to respond with, "how could I *not* dream of you," or something fucking cheesy like, "baby, let's make that dream a reality," but I didn't. I responded with nothing except a boyish "goodnight."

"I'll find you tomorrow," she said with a purr.

"Don't..."

"Don't?"

"Don't miss me." I grinned.

"Foolish." Maude sashayed out of the billiards room. The two husbands drooled at her figure as she went, both of them undoubtedly to be slapped by their wives later. *God help them... God help me.* The red rug complimented her lips as she looked back once and was gone.

I stood there searching for the piece of me that walked away with her. I had to see her again, not only because she was a goddess, but because I had to get that piece back, and more. The cigar was dying between my fingers just as the night was. I took one final puff and looked into the hallway again. Luther, Owen, and the goon platoon walked past the billiards room without noticing me. It was amazing that any of them could walk in a semi-straight line. While in motion Luther's high was so obvious that it wouldn't have surprised me if, at any moment, he floated up the rear staircase and into his bed. They eventually reached the steps and I could hear their shoes pattering upwards.

But one man did notice me. He paused in front of the billiards room and fixed his stare on me. He wasn't one of the men at Irvin's table; he must have been seated at the other one. He had the same desperate look of a man gagged and tied to train tracks. The whistle was blowing and he couldn't move. He couldn't communicate.

"Jay!" One of the mobsters out of my frame of vision barked back to him.

"Jay, let's go! Stop lollygaggin'!"

He looked like he wanted to tell me something, perhaps a warning. There was something he knew that ate at his undigested dinner. He twitched at the sound of the voice in front of him, shivering at some invisible breeze that brushed by.

*What is it, Jay? What's eating you?*

I held my tongue. Clearly, Jay was the black sheep of the family I had met at dinner. He didn't belong. I couldn't decipher whether that was good or bad for him. All I knew was that whoever Jay was, he was better than the rest of them. He said goodbye with a blink and disappeared in the direction of the back stairs.

I dropped my cigar stump into an empty vase and surrendered to the night. I took the long way back to my room, retracing Maude's steps and avoiding the path taken by the gangsters. The climb up the mountainous red stairs seemed never-ending. I began to realize just how profoundly tired I was. I had slept face down on my desk in Brooklyn the night before. Then, there was the drive and, of course, the drinking. There was Maude and Luther and something in the air that felt like quicksand. I reached the third floor and regretted taking the long route.

The corridor rocked from side to side and for a moment I felt myself back on a ship returning from Europe. Returning from a muddy war. *Fuck* the war. I hate war. I hated the feeling, when I unlocked my door, of being on the brink of chaos.

My room was dark and I left it that way. I fumbled about in the moonlight, removing my clothes and drinking two swallows from the bottle of gin. I found the .38 Smith & Wesson in my suitcase and looked at it. It had two barrels, two triggers, and two hands holding it. The room moved just as my apartment had. The bottle hit my lips again and I wobbled to the side of the bed, sat down and cradled the gun in my hands as if it was some lethal newborn. Somewhere inside of it there was a bullet – alone, like me. I asked myself if it wanted to escape.

Outside the lawn was vacant, the ocean was still and calm, lit by half a moon, the other half was elsewhere. My body sank under the covers. I rolled away from the gun and then back to it. Away and then back.

I reached for the .38 as it smiled at me beneath the bisected moon. My middle finger touched the butt of the pistol and I felt your hand. Your hands were always so warm, like small oven mitts. The hand I felt now was cold. But it was *yours*. You stopped my fingers from coiling around the gun.

"Don't," you whispered.

"Why?" I asked.

"Save them."

"Save who, Anna?"

"Save them."

You were gone again.

The smell of your perfume lingered, whisking me to sleep.

# 12.

I didn't dream of Maude as she requested. I dreamt of Anna without remembering much of it. I only recalled her nose, long eyelashes and her touch, all in fragments. I saw the crease on her chin and thought about all the years and lines on her face I would never see form.

It rained overnight. Even if I didn't look out the window and see the damp grass I still would have felt it in my bones. The .38 remained on the nightstand. I stood and swiped the gun from the table, looking at it once before tossing it back into my luggage. My eyes found the bottle of gin. My head was splitting in half as a reminder not to touch it, as if I needed a reminder. If the bottle possessed a wider mouth I'm fairly certain it would have laughed at me. I screwed the cap on and rolled it into one of the dresser drawers.

The shower, however cramped, woke me up more than anything. My brown suit I wore the night before would suffice, minus the vest and tie. The hands of my watch pointed to three minutes past eight. I knew only two things: I needed to eat and I needed to take a long walk. Walks helped me in the city; I figured it would probably work wonders in a place such as Newport.

I retrieved my pea coat from a hook beside the door and left the room, locking it out of instinct. The back stairs guided me to the first floor where a large sign at the entrance to the ballroom revealed that there was a breakfast buffet. I could have wept tears of joy right there, but I refrained.

The Hermann Hotel took on a different persona in the daytime. At night it was a monumental white ghost of a mansion set in contrast to the dark Atlantic behind it. Walking inside The Herm after the sunset felt like an exploration through the organs of some mythical whale that contained the secrets of the universe. During the day The Herm looked more like an outcast of heaven, not out of enmity, but simply because it didn't fit. The Hermann was here, in the sunlight, because the angels ran out of room.

Secrets were still present during the day; I could feel them in the walls, only now they were suppressed by celestial light that seemed to pour in from every direction. Yellow and white rays knifed through most windows and bounced off the polished floor, causing me to squint.

The ballroom was more crowded than the night before, perhaps with early arrivals for the Harvest Festival Ball, which, I quickly remembered, was *this* evening. It was Saturday already and I wasn't prepared for an influx of people and noise. *Had I known about the damn party, I doubt I would have even come here this weekend.*

En route to the buffet, I managed to intercept one of the waiters and asked him if I could pay now and take my breakfast into the morning room. He kindly replied that it shouldn't be a problem. I slipped him some cash, loaded up my plate with just about everything the buffet had to offer, and scrammed out of the area before I was forced to talk to anyone else.

The morning room was designed to grant as much sun as possible into it. The area was coated in a tangerine tint, that initiated a feeling of warmth, which began to melt away my hangover. I sat in a plush chair with the food, juice, and coffee in front of me on a low ornate table. I ate faster than I could breathe and quickly began to feel better. Soon, I leaned back, pregnant with satisfaction. There was an oil painting on the wall near the fireplace in front of me, one of many like it. This one was of an older woman, who looked down at me in distain as if she had just caught me fondling her royal poodle inappropriately. I would have told her to calm down or loosen up, but I figured the poor hag was stuck that way, just as I was stuck in that chair, immobilized by a buffet.

I must have sat there for a half an hour, part of it covered by a blink of a nap, before I finally found the will to get up. I returned my plate, glasses, and silverware to the ballroom and donned my coat. The red carpet muffled my shoes as I traversed the main lobby and exited the front of The Hermann.

Above me the sky was locked in a struggle to clear up, the sun poking holes through the grayness only to be sealed by more clouds. The air retained a damp chill that gave it teeth, especially when the wind became disgruntled. I walked without a destination in mind, with no purpose other than to clear my head and finish the job the morning room started. The sidewalk was layered with dead leaves. I shuffled through them at a carefree pace, the sound similar to turning a radio dial through static.

At the end of the block I paused next to a street lamp and lit a cigar. A red and cream colored Chrysler Imperial rolled by me, the inside packed with overzealous partygoers arriving *way* ahead of schedule. I walked another block, smoking the stogie as I went. The ground was no longer paved beneath my feet. I looked down and then off to my left to see a dirt road that seemed to flow nowhere but somewhere all at once. It was the type of road that is so small and beaten that it was difficult to distinguish from a wide path. Whatever it was, it was familiar to me. With a puff of cigar smoke I disappeared down the trail like a magician. I was encased in barren, sleeping trees. The sun still fought to touch me, contending now with both clouds and branches. I blew out more smoke and kicked stones as I went.

The path went straight for a long time and then began to curve here and there until I realized I was moving away from the ocean. The trail had brought me to one of the rear corners of the Homespun Inn. It had happened again. It had summoned me down the path like a magnet. It spun me into its web and smothered my wings.

I made my way around to the face of the small, two-story brick building that resembled something out of a children's book. The black shutters and doors were somehow welcoming. Smoke rose from one of the chimneys and gamboled over the roof and away. One of the front doors suddenly creaked open. A couple, younger than me, walked down the steps. The child between them was perhaps four, maybe five. He clung to one hand of each parent and laughed as they lifted him into the air. I stood there, a spectator, until I was propelled back in time again.

I'm standing in front of the Homespun and the weather is not quite as raspy. In this memory I'm not alone. You're beside me, Anna. You press your shoulder against mine as we look at the inn. It looks back at us.

"Will you build me a house that looks like this someday?" you ask.

I laugh like a teenager and turn to you. "I would build you a castle with an elevator to heaven if I could, and I wouldn't do it *someday,* I would do it now."

"Is that a fact, baby?"

"I wouldn't joke about such a thing," I reply.

"It would take you a long time."

"It would take me a day."

You laugh at that. "You're crazy," you say with a kiss, brushing your finger over my scar.

"You're with me." I wrap my arms around you.

"I would never want a boring man."

"I should certainly hope not."

There's a family in front of the inn. The parents are off under a tree talking with another couple. Two children are playing catch with a purple ball; neither of them is older than six. The larger of the two throws the ball too fast and too high. It bounces near my feet. Before I can bend down and pick it up, the smaller boy is sprinting to the ball. His tiny foot gets caught on a root or a rock and he falls, scraping his cheek on something. The boy begins crying almost instantly. I move towards him in a flash, turn him over gently and look at the cut on his face between the crocodile tears.

"You're okay, buddy! You're okay!" I say to him as if he's my own son.

"It hurts!" The boy says.

"Just a scratch, kiddo, just a scratch."

The boy smiles at me the way kids do when they realize the world isn't ending. His parents on the other side of the lawn, if they are his parents, remain oblivious. "Where is your Mommy and Daddy?" I ask him.

He points to the chatting adults.

"C'mon, buddy, lets go."

I scoop him up in my arms and carry him back to his parents. You walk with me and I hand the boy off to them. They thank me profusely and comfort the boy. I tell them they don't need to thank me. As we walk away, I can feel you looking at me. I turn and see that faint Anna-smile painted above your cleft chin. We say nothing because we know we are both thinking the same thing. We are both realizing the same thing and falling in love with the idea of something *more.* All I can do in this moment is smile back at you. My smile is only a fraction as beautiful, that much I am sure of. I smile at you now as the memory turns gray, like the sky. You reach out to me and when you do your image fades the way grains of sand flee from smooth stones in a brash wind.

From a few feet away, a sentence hummed through the air at me. "I know that look well," said Maude. I knew it was her before I could turn to confirm it. She wore a long coat as dark as mine, a red scarf, and an olive-colored beret over her golden locks. Her feline eyes peered out beneath two blonde curls as her ruby lips pursed against the cold.

"What look?" I asked.

"The look of someone chasing ghosts."

"There's no such thing as ghosts."

"Only the ones you want to haunt you." She stepped towards me in slow strides.

"I love this place," she said. "It's quaint and warm compared to most of the... uh... *cottages* around here."

We both let out a little laugh at the irony.

Maude continued, "I would have stayed here. *Should* have stayed at the Homespun. Woulda gotten *some* peace and quiet."

"Funny," I said, "I took you for a flapper."

"I tried that. It was too easy. Besides, even my breed needs some peace." She flashed a cheery smirk and looked back at the Homespun. "There's just something about this place that reminds me of my grandparents' home in Pennsylvania."

"Reminds you of a different life?"

"Yeah... a past life maybe." She nodded.

We gazed at the building and then back to each other.

"What does it remind you of?" Maude finally asked.

"It reminds me of what could have been."

"Do your memories smile back?"

"Some of them do," I said.

"Then not all is lost. Stop looking so grumpy."

"I'm not grumpy," I laughed nervously at how razor sharp she was. "Did you follow me here?" I moved closer to her.

"Don't flatter yourself, Emmett Roane."

I gave her a curious look as I tried to find my verbal footing. "Frankly, doll, it's too early and I'm too hungover for this amount of sass."

"Frankly, I don't give a damn what you can and cannot handle," she said. "Walk with me." It was an order, not a request.

I sighed at the sky and tried to remember how to place one foot in front of the other. We walked.

~

Luther Irvin sat up in bed. He had slept later than most of his men because he'd stayed awake later the night before. His white undershirt was stained with drool from his diced lip. He found a handkerchief on the nightstand and wiped the corner of his mouth. As usual, Owen and Wallace were seated nearby. Wallace sorted papers on a coffee table while Owen struggled to comprehend the funny pages of the local news. Nicky entered the room, his short, stout cup of coffee oddly resembling his own form.

"Late start today, heh, boss?" Nicky said.

Luther said nothing. He sat up further in bed, positioning his back against the headboard.

"Mista Irvin, I got to thinkin' that maybe today we head downtown. Buddy of mine told me a while back where we might be able to find some whores. Whuddya say? Eh? Whuddya say? My fuckin' cock is fuckin' itchin."

"Sounds like a personal problem," said Luther as he rubbed his eyes.

"I don't mean itchin' like I, uh, caught, uh, somethin'. I mean itchin' like bored, boss."

"Nicky, how's about you do something useful with your life and fetch me a cup of coffee with a pinch of absinthe?"

Nicky pointed to Owen and Wallace. "Why can't they get it?"

"Because they are *busy*, Nicky! Do as I ask!"

"Fine, fine," the tubby man replied.

"And bring me the fucking Clarinet while you're at it!"

"Fine, boss!" Nicky turned around and exited the room.

Luther's high from the previous night was gone. His anemic body and blue face shivered as the bed sheets slipped away from him. A moment later Nicky returned with the requested cup and the clarinet case. He laid the case down on the bed beside Luther and walked around to the nightstand, where he set the saucer down and stirred the mixture once more for good measure. Luther brought the cup to his broken lip. It took only a single sip for him to explode into rage.

"What the *hell* is this?"

"Heh, sir?" Nicky looked shocked.

"I said, '*what* the *hell* is *this*?'"

"Coffee, Mr. Irv. With a pinch of absi – "

"Exactly! A *pinch* of absinthe! Not three fingers of it! You poured too much, you fucking hump!"

"Sir... Mr. Irv. I'm sorry, sir..."

"Get this bullshit out of my face!" Luther screamed and threw the full cup at Nicky. It bounced off his gut and sprayed liquid down his vest.

"I'm sorry, sir." Nicky bent down and picked up the cup from the stained rug. Owen and Wallace sat frozen by the boss's outburst.

Luther held his face in his hands until his breathing returned to normal. "No... I'm sorry, Nicky. Just leave. Just go."

The round man slowly backed out of the room.

"Close the door behind you, Nicky."

Nicky latched it shut and the room returned to a spooky calm.

Owen rose from the couch and walked over to Luther, handing him his own cup of coffee. "Here, boss, you can have mine. I barely touched it."

"Thank you, Owen. You are so kind."

Wallace stared at Luther, his thick glasses acting as a pair of magnifying lenses searching for the fine print. "What is it, Luther?"

"What is *what*, Wallace?"

"What is the problem? There is something else going on here."

"My dear Wallace, how astute you truly are." Luther sipped Owen's coffee. "Yes... there is *something.*"

"Sir?" Owen stepped closer again.

"We... have a rather paramount problem. Lock the door,

Owen."

Owen did as he was asked and then returned his full attention to Luther.

"I've had some suspicions about our Jay for some time now," the boss began. "At first I merely thought he was a softy or a dumbbell... or even a faggot. Something was *off.* All these detriments may still hold true, but he has one more characteristic that cannot be tolerated. He's a fucking *rat.*"

"A *rat,* boss? Jay?" Owen shook his head.

"Yes, Jay is the rat of rats," Luther lisped.

"On what grounds do you base this?" Wallace asked.

"On the grounds that while all of you mugs were asleep last night having wet dreams, I took it upon myself to go through Jay's shit."

"And...?" Wallace dug.

"And... what I found inside the pocket of his jacket were not one but *two* hand-written letters, one meant for Frank Norelli and the other intended for the police. *Both* letters coughed up our entire plan for Sunday, see. Jay's getting cold feet and intends to blow the lid off the entire show."

Wallace shook his head quietly and beamed down at the table. Owen scratched his hairless scalp and looked about the room, befuddled.

"Holy shit," the giant muttered. "Fucking *rat.*"

"Fucking *rat.*" Luther hummed.

"Agreed," Wallace said. "Do you have said letters?"

"I put them back," Luther answered. "I didn't want him to suspect us and scurry off to Norelli or the authorities and spill the beans in person."

"Indeed," Wallace said.

"I'll kill him. I'll do it right now." Owen's face was red.

"No you won't, and not right now either. I'll have Carmelo take him out to the cliffs and whack him out there. Dump his ratty ass into the ocean. We'll tell Jay there's a bootlegger coming to shore that needs to be met. Carmelo has been itching for blood ever since Norelli bumped him and Alonzo out of the family, so I'll give the wop a bone on this one."

"Very well," Owen responded.

The three men sat quietly as Luther opened up the clarinet case and assembled the opium pipe. He loaded the shaft and sparked the drug. The world became lighter again. Smoke crept from Luther's jagged scar and hooked up to the ceiling, forming a grim reaper's sickle.

"Wallace," Luther beckoned in a feathery voice.

"Yes?"

"Bring Carmelo in here now, discreetly. We'll provide him with instructions. Get it over with. We have a party to attend later."

Wallace abandoned his papers and entered the adjoining room.

~

Maude and I strolled into the trees and down another rough path. Every few footsteps her coat brushed against mine, sending electricity into my spine.

"So, did you have fun last night?" she inquired.

"Yes, as a matter of fact, I did."

"You don't sound too sure."

"I'm sure of it."

"You haven't met anyone like me, am I right?"

"You're not wrong, Maude Mable."

"I had fun, too, aside from the gangster rendezvous. You just *had* to go and be popular."

"Well, now we know not to play with them."

"I *already* knew that, good sir. You just felt the need to find out for yourself. You're like a child who is told that a stove is hot, yet you have to touch it and burn yourself."

"I didn't *burn* myself."

"Yet," she said. "You're trouble."

"Than why are you walking around with me?"

"Someone has to keep you in line," she chirped.

"Whatever you say, lady. Where are we going anyway?"

"I would venture to say that when you left the hotel earlier you didn't have a destination in mind. Why does a destination matter now?"

"It doesn't. I'm just curious."

"We're going to the cliff walk, handsome, but first I have to show you something."

"Cliff walk?"

"Yes, Emmett. Do you live under a rock? It's marvelous."

"I've only been to Newport once before."

"Well, you're missing out. You'll thank me later."

"I certainly hope so." I bit my lower lip.

She rolled her eyes at that one.

"You're taking me to the cliffs so you can dump me into the ocean, aren't you?" I joked.

"I would never. You're too much fun, despite being so grumpy."

I exhaled audibly. "I'm not grumpy. This is just how I look all the time. And what is it you have to show me before the cliffs?" I asked.

"So many questions. Are you a detective?"

"Not from what I can deduce."

"Just be quiet then. You'll see."

Maude took my hand, enclosing my icy fingers in warmth. We dipped down a smaller, narrower path.

"Maude, *where?*"

"Shhh." She held a finger to her lips. "Shut it!"

I felt as though I was fifteen years younger. We came upon a fence that had been severed by a fallen tree. Whatever storm had felled it happened some time ago. The tree was old and rotted but still provided an opening into some *other* world on the opposite side. With the help of a rock Maude climbed onto the horizontal tree, balancing herself tentatively, one foot in front of the other.

"This is someone's private property, isn't it?" I asked rhetorically.

"Maybe."

"So it is."

"You gonna follow me or not?"

"Fine, fine, fine." I climbed up and followed her through the fence until we were undoubtedly in somebody's backyard. "My best friend warned me not to get arrested this weekend," I said.

"I take that with the smallest grain of salt coming from you – the guy I met after he punched out a feller in The Hermann's speak."

"Uhhh – yeah. Good point there, madam."

"Do I look like a damn madam to you?"

"I guess not. We're not gonna catch flak for this? We aren't supposed to be here."

"Hardly anyone is here in the colder months. These are mostly summer homes."

I looked across the lawn and saw what appeared to be a garden with dozens of strangely shaped plantings. Their rich summer green was now faded to a deadened brown.

"What is that over there?" I nodded in the garden's direction.

"*That* is where we are going, mister."

It was a garden unlike any I had ever seen. Maude walked me between hedges and bushes sculpted into animals, geometric figures, and ornamental designs. We moved side by side, separating around some of the larger sculptures only to return to each another on the other side.

"You look intrigued," Maude said. "I hinted that it was special."

I gazed around at the hedges, some of them three feet tall, others ten feet, and everything in between. An elephant, a lion, a dog, a bear and its cub. A camel, a giraffe, a unicorn, and a big bad wolf. There were designs that arched over paths and spiraled up to the sky. It was a world of wonderment on the brink of hibernation. "Fascinating," I turned back to her.

"I know. It's called a topiary garden. Over seventy pieces. It's been like this since 1905," said Maude. "Not many people know about it."

"How did you know about this place?" I asked. I felt almost angry: the garden was right under my nose last time I was in Newport and I never saw it with Anna.

Maude grazed her fingers across the side of the lion and ambled over to me. "When I was a girl my father used to bring me here. He was good friends with the superintendent – the man responsible for creating and maintaining these beauties. My father would sit on the far side of the garden. Sometimes he would look out at the ocean, sometimes he would look toward the animals… or plants, I suppose. Sometimes he would read, sometimes he would write, sometimes he would paint. He was an artist, through and through. I was just too young to appreciate it. He passed away from cancer when I was thirteen. Whenever I'm in Newport I try to sneak in here. I think… I think maybe he's here sometimes."

"Maybe he is," I said, holding the weight of her words.

"I would run around these things and pretend they were real," she said, laughing at some incoming recollection. "One time I decided to climb up the unicorn thinking I could ride it. I sat on it," she giggled into the breeze, " and when I did I fell right through the branches!"

We both laughed at the imagery. I could feel the flame inside my chest again, small, flickering, but existent.

"I ripped my dress and killed the unicorn."

"He looks fine now… aside from the brown spots," I said through fading laughter.

"I was such a brat that day. My father gave up on whatever he was working on and just sat me on his lap. He could never stay mad at me, though. He sat me on his lap and began ripping out pages from his notebook, showing me how to make perfect paper airplanes. We probably let a hundred of them fly out over the garden. All of them went far. The last plane we threw was taken by the wind, up and away. I never saw where it crashed."

"I don't think it ever crashed," I said. "I think it's traveling the world. Any day it's gonna find its way back to you, and when it does it will have one hell of a story to tell."

"You think so?"

"I know so."

"I hope," she laughed. The more I heard that laugh, the more I realized how easily it drew a smile up my face the way sails rise on a ship's mast.

"I hope," she said again.

"All you can do."

Maude and I stayed in the garden for a while, flirting back and forth amongst the animals, wishing they were real and pretending they were listening to us. Just before we departed for the cliff walk Maude asked me which sculpture was my favorite.

"The big bad wolf," I told her.

"How do you know he's bad?" she asked.

"Because it takes one to know one."

# 13.

Carmelo stepped out of The Hermann Hotel and slicked his dark hair back with a comb. His fedora was pulled over his ears, locking the hair in place. He returned the comb to one side of his coat as his free hand disappeared into the other side. He found the pocket pistol and took it out. The gun, no bigger than the length of his hand, glinted in the day's gray light like a silver dollar. Carmelo pulled back the slide to chamber a .25 caliber round. His instructions were clear and he was ready. He never liked Jay much anyway.

Even as a refugee from the Norelli family, Carmelo managed to fit in with Irvin's crew. Jay never did. Furthermore, Jay was now a rat, and rats had to go. Carmelo heard someone behind him exit the hotel and quickly slipped the pocket pistol back into its abode. It was Jay.

"So the booze is coming onto the beach? In broad daylight?" he asked Carmelo.

"Yeah, the cliffs," Carmelo responded coldly.

"During the day?" Jay put on his hat.

"Yes, during the fucking day. Keep your voice down."

Jay buttoned his coat. "How come the boss is only sending us two to take this thing?"

"Boss heard there's just one small shipment coming in on a baby rum-runner. Only two guys on this thing. Two guys for two guys. We kill 'em and take the crates, just like Owen and Nicky did yesterday."

"I ain't ever heard of rum-runners coming into this area," Jay said.

Carmelo lit a cigarette. "They do, all the time."

"I'm surprised," said Jay. "Figured the boss would wanna lay low for the rest of the weekend. Stay quiet before the storm. You know?"

"Mr. Irvin don't stay quiet for nothin'. You should know that by now, numb nuts. Even when he claims to want silence, he's screaming at hell to rise."

"Yeah, yeah."

"You got your piece on you?" Carmelo asked.

"Of course."

"All right." Carmelo took a hefty drag of the cig. "Lets fuckin' go before we miss our chance. Then we're *both* dead."

He stayed about a foot behind Jay as they walked, keeping one eye on him in the event that he suddenly became wise and pulled his own pistol. Luckily for Carmelo, Jay wasn't very wise. The two walked and barely spoke. The path they took led straight to a stone passage, which opened up to the ocean and the cliffs before it.

~

I followed Maude out of the topiary garden and back over the lawn. We exited the busted fence from which we came and made our way back to the main path. The ocean became louder, the wind more formidable. The dirt turned into sand and rock.

"Watch your step out here," she said. "It may look like a piece of cake at first but it gets a little precarious."

"Precarious? You do know that I was in the military, right?"

"You didn't tell me that. During the war?"

I didn't answer, allowing the thudding of the waves to crush any response she may have expected. The cliff walk began as a cemented path braced by stone walls or railings. It was easy and the view stunning. Maybe I *would* thank Maude later.

It's a rare thing to be on the edge of the ocean without standing on a beach. It became more surreal when the obvious path ended and we truly were walking on the cliff. Our conversation dwindled as we concentrated on our footing, avoiding crevasses and deep puddles left from the night before. The puddles behaved like broken mirrors fallen from above. It felt like the cliff was not a cliff but a barrier made by God, separating us from the unknown.

Maude and I moved over the rocky terrain with the determination of two ants on a gravel driveway. Occasionally a silent seagull swooped over the lead-colored water that reflected the overcasting sky. Now and then, the sun would peek at us before being pulled behind the curtain of clouds. Maude detoured down to one of the lower boulders and waited for me. When I reached her she was looking out at the turbulent surf. What she was gazing at easily equated, even harmonized with whatever was going on within her soul.

"Tell me about your father," she said. "I told you about mine."

"My father?"

"Yes."

I thought in silence for a moment before I found what I was looking for.

"My father is a real character. He has this way about him, a dry sarcasm that makes everyone in the room laugh. He has a heart bigger than a watermelon. The man rarely smiles, but when he does, you know it. He never raised a hand to me, I think its because his father was abusive. My mother on the other hand, she's a different story. Not one to be tested. God bless her." I chuckled.

"Give me a memory," said Maude.

"A memory? Hmmm, well…" I picked up the flattest rock I could find and hurled it, side arm, over the water. It skipped over the rough waves three times before it sank.

"I was in Long Beach Island, New Jersey, on vacation with my family. I was little. My Pops brought me to the beach. For about an hour he tried to teach me how to skip a stone over the water. I couldn't do it. Tried and tried. Couldn't do it. I finally threw it as hard as I could and the stone skipped three, four, maybe even five times. It wasn't until I was older that I realized that my father threw that stone from behind me. It was *his* stone that bounced so well, not mine. He made me feel like I was a champion."

Maude grinned as her eyes traveled to mine. "I like that one," she said.

"So do I."

"How did you finally learn to do it?"

"It just came to me one day."

I took Maude's hand and helped her down from the boulder. We ascended another set of rocks and headed in the direction of what I assumed was a tunnel connecting one side of the cliff walk to the other beneath a patch of earth. I felt a sense of foreboding coming from that tunnel. I didn't like what was in there or perhaps just beyond the opposite end.

~

Carmelo eyed the nebulous opening of the tunnel only a few feet away from him. The blackness stared back at him with abhorrence for what he was about to do. Jay stood on his other side, scanning the water for a rum-running craft that didn't exist.

"I don't see nothin', Carmelo."

*And you won't,* Carmelo almost blurted.

"You sure this is the spot?" Jay continued.

"Oh yeah, this is the spot."

"They must be late."

"Any second now." Carmelo extracted two cigarettes from his case and snapped it closed, the sharp sound startling Jay out of his pensive pose. "Have a smoke, Jay. It'll do ya good."

"Sure," Jay said.

Carmelo handed him the cig and sparked a light. The salty wind swept between them and killed the flame on the first attempt, doused it on the second, and allowed it to live on the third. Carmelo shielded the lighter with his hand and put the fire to his own cigarette after lighting Jay's. Smoke drifts made their way over the rocks and squandered before reaching the air above the white caps.

"Hey, Ja, ya ever hear the joke about the Irish guy with no legs?"

"Nahh, I think I'da remembered that one."

"Well, I'll tell yus." Carmelo looked in both directions to ensure they were alone.

"Shoot away," said Jay.

"So, this Irish guy with no legs is laying on the beach on a lovely day. He's just there, somehow, alone, enjoying himself. He has an umbrella over himself, of course, otherwise he'd get fuckin' roasted. Anyways these three gorgeous dames walk by and they sees this poor mick alone with no legs. So they walk up to him. The first one bends down and asks the mick if he's ever been hugged. The mick says 'no, no, I've never been hugged.' So she bends down and gives him a hug. He says 'thank you, thank you.' The second dame bends down and asks the mick if he's ever been kissed. He says, 'no, no, I've never been kissed.' So, naturally, she bends down and gives him a kiss. The mick thanks her repeatedly, tells her, 'this is the happiest day of my life.' Finally, the third dame bends down and asks the mick, 'have you ever been fucked?' He says, 'no, no, of course not.' She stands up, still lookin' at him, and says, 'you're about to be... *the tide's coming in.*'"

Jay was still laughing hysterically at the joke when Carmelo walked behind him, pulled the pocket pistol, and put one bullet in the back of his skull. The shot resonated through the salty mist. Jay dropped forward, his body now uninhabited on the edge of the cliff.

~

I knew it was a gunshot because I'd heard that sound so many times before. Maude would have been better off if she was walking the cliffs with a different man, one who would have taken her in the opposite direction of danger. But that wasn't me. Earlier I was hesitant to sneak into a garden; now I was heading towards a potential bullet. I guess the garden just wasn't risky enough.

The mouth of the tunnel was roughly two meters in diameter and bricked into an arch that was covered in bright green algae. We were right in front of it when the gunshot echoed out of the pitch black.

"What was that?" Maude looked at me and then at the tunnel.

"I don't know." It was a lie. I didn't want to frighten her. I gazed at the opening, the darkness, just as intently as she did. "You in the mood to investigate?"

"Always," she came back, with a puckish smile.

I felt my pockets for a book of matches, found one and held it out by my waist.

"Don't be a fool, Emmett." Maude produced a heavy lighter and gave it to me. "Get with the times, old man."

"Thanks." I thumbed the igniter, allowing the fire to come out and dance.

My right hand held the light out in front of us while my left hand grasped Maude's. We entered the tunnel.

"Are you *sure* you're not a detective?"

"Yeah, doll, I'm pretty positive."

We had walked only a few feet before we descended a brief set of stairs. The passage was now completely starved of light other than the source I held fluctuating in front of us. I navigated between pools of stagnant water. The dank air grew thicker around us. We reached a bend in the tunnel and the brick walls became a ribbed metallic surface. A rat darted out of a hole, bounced off my foot, and scurried between Maude's legs into the shallow water behind us.

"Jesus!" Maude gasped.

"Don't mind him," I said calmly, numb from months of sleeping, eating, and breathing alongside rats in the trenches of

Europe. Damned creatures.

Maude and I could see the end of the tunnel now. The sun, while overcast, was still blindingly white. The ground became dry as we ramped up to the opening.

A man stood near the edge of the cliff. That part was fine; a man can stand wherever he pleases. The problem was that he was standing over a dead body, smoking a cigarette and smiling. The back of corpse's head was coated in fresh blood. It streamed down his ears and onto the rocks.

"Oh my god! What – ?" Maude's voice was silenced by my hand. I pulled her to my chest, snuffed out the lighter, and pressed both of our bodies into the wall to make us less visible.

He was one of Luther Irvin's men, but his hat wouldn't allow me to pinpoint which one. I only knew he wasn't one of the ones I'd met.

Maude's voice vibrated into my palm. I whispered in her ear, "Maude, Maude Maude, listen to me… you cannot scream. You have to stay quiet. If he sees us, he'll kill us. We are witnesses now."

She nodded.

"If I take my hand away will you stay quiet?"

She nodded again. My hand parted from Maude's lips only to be replaced by her own. She held onto me as if we would fall off the Earth otherwise.

The gangster rolled the dead man over onto his back. I could see his face now. He was the man who had so strangely paused in front of the billiards room at the conclusion of last night. He looked up at the sky now, offering it the same expression he'd directed at me when I saw him alive. His coat flapped open as the hit man searched his body for something important. I could see a piece of paper slip from the dead man's inside pocket and catch the wind with a mind of its own. It sailed onto a sharp rock and stuck there, waiting. The gangster was about to chase the paper down when my foot loosened a rock and sent it clattering between Maude and me. *Son of a bitch, how in the hell could I be so clumsy?*

The hit man turned like a shark sensing a drop of blood in water. He removed a compact handgun from inside his coat and pointed it at the tunnel.

"Emmett," Maude breathed desperately.

We inched backwards until I found an alcove barely big enough to conceal the two of us. We tucked our bodies inside. The gangster breached the tunnel's lips, the outside light pouring around him, creating a villainous silhouette. He plucked the cigarette butt from his mouth and discarded it.

"Hello! Anyone there?"

Silence. He walked further in.

"Anyone hiding? Come out if you want to play."

The wind howled into the passage. Silence again.

"I ain't afraid to use a stitch of force to *pry* you out, whoever you are."

His frame became aligned with our alcove.

"I ain't afraid," he said once more.

I reached out and latched onto his gun hand with a vice-like grip.

"Good," I growled. "Neither am I."

My free hand emerged from the shadows in the form of a battering ram. I hit his jaw, feeling it wrench out of place. The blow pushed him completely off balance. I used the surprise to knock the petite pistol from his grasp, sending it airborne back towards the tunnel's opening. The pistol bounced off the ribbed wall and landed in a patch of light. I made a point to watch where it landed. The mobster, noticing my concentration was off of him, seized the opportunity to land a punch on the side of my head. He wound up again and I tilted my head so that he connected with the top of my skull. Knowing my own thick-headedness, I wouldn't have been surprised if the connection broke his hand. He shrieked in pain and knocked me into the wall, sending some of the wind out of me.

"Emmett!" Maude screamed.

I looked up in time to see the glimmer of what she was worried about. The goon had a stiletto knife. The blade sliced the air in front of my face, first one way and then the other. I dodged him again and again. His arm shot at my stomach in a stabbing motion. I moved just in time and simultaneously struck his knife-wielding hand, derailing the attack. The blade hit the metallic wall and broke in half. My fists alternated into his face and gut, repelling him away from me. The broken stiletto blade lay at my foot. I knelt down, gripped it, the sharp edge cutting my palm, and jammed it into the monster's side. He let out another wild shriek of pain. He threw punches that I blocked. I threw punches that he didn't, driving him to the end of the tunnel.

Before he could become cognizant of the gun within his reach, I kicked him square in the chest as hard as fucking possible. He aviated backwards and landed partially on top of the corpse on the edge of the cliff. His hands began to frantically search the dead man's clothing for something.

He found it, a Savage Model 1907. A struggle ensued against the weapon's holster. When he finally freed the pistol, I was already aiming his own gun at him.

"Don't miss me," I said.

I fired five shots, every bullet entering him, ending him. His body twisted as he screamed shrilly one last time. The gangster tumbled over the side of the cliff and into eternity.

The weapon I held in my right hand was hot and empty. My left hand was bleeding from handling the broken blade. Both of my hands were trembling. I looked over my shoulder at Maude. She held her hands up near her ears, her stance inadvertently framing a pale expression of terror.

"You... shot him," she said. "You *killed* him."

"Absolutely," I answered sharply, as if the war had ended only yesterday.

We both knew another war had just begun.

"You *killed* him," she repeated.

"It was us or him."

"Lord..." her breathing was labored.

Maude leaned against the edge of the tunnel, catching her breath and struggling to process what had just occurred. Her teary golden eyes swept over the ocean, fishing for a way to wash down such a bitter pill.

"I've never seen anyone die before," she said. "Not... not like that."

"I know you haven't." I tossed the pocket gun over the cliff. I figured the hit man would have wanted it back.

"You killed him so *easily*."

"Not as easily as he killed this poor sap," I retorted.

"They were both Luther Irvin's men?"

"Yes," I squatted next to the remaining dead body without knowing what it was that I needed to find. My eyes drifted left and I noticed the paper still wedged between two rocks nearby, beckoning me closer as it thrashed in the wind. I approached it cautiously so I wouldn't scare it away.

My voice carried back to Maude as I closed the distance. "They were both Irvin's boys. The question is: why was one out here to smoke the other?"

"Maybe they were both dipping into the same honeypot," Maude said.

"Honeypot?"

"Woman. Maybe they were both sleeping with the same – "

"No," I interrupted, "that wasn't it at all."

I freed the paper from the rocks and examined it. It was a letter, moist and battered, but still legible. What I read chilled the blood in my veins and froze my arteries before I could even reach the last sentence. I remained crouched in silence, waves of horror and disbelief inside my head thrashing just as the whitecaps did below. I thought I had known about the evil that can thrive in man and the extremes that such a force can drive him to. I was wrong.

"Emmett." Maude parted from the tunnel and came closer to me.

I couldn't speak.

"Emmett... what is it?"

I couldn't breath.

"Please don't scare me any more than I already am."

"We have to go. We have to go right *now*." I stood.

"Go where?"

"Off this cliff. The man who wrote this, *that man*," I pointed to the body, " was killed for *this.* " I held up the letter. "The man who killed him, the one I just shot into a nose dive, was supposed to be back by now. They'll send someone sniffing around soon."

I folded the letter and put it in my pocket.

"What does it say?"

"When we're safe, Maude, not now."

I returned to the body, knelt down on the rock, and rolled it to the edge. "We can't leave anything for them to find out here." The heavy mass of what was formally life fell into the water.

"The bodies…" Maude said. "They'll wash up somewhere, won't they?"

"By then it won't matter. I hope."

I hunted for bullet shells, found a few, and sent them over the cliff.

"What about the blood?" Maude made a point.

"I forgot to bring a mop with me when I left the room this morning, gorgeous."

I untucked my shirt and ripped it into a long, thin strip.

"You're making a mop?"

"A bandage," I said, as I wrapped it around my sliced palm. With my other hand I took Maude by the arm. "We are *leaving.*"

In the distance Maude and I could see a way off the cliff walk. We wasted no time in getting there.

~

Most of Luther Irvin's men were downstairs eating breakfast. All that remained in the three connecting rooms were Wallace, Owen, and of course, Luther himself, who had ordered breakfast to be delivered. The boss was fully clothed in his three-piece charcoal suit, pinstripes and immaculate shoes included. The opium levitated him over to the window. He licked his gashed lip before sipping more tea, this time with the *correct* amount of absinthe.

"Carmelo should have returned by now," said Luther. "I don't like how this tastes."

"The tea, Mr. Irvin?" Owen said.

"No, this *situation.* Carmelo should have been back already."

Wallace raised his head from a table of papers. "Their destination wasn't exactly nearby. Perhaps the walk is taking longer than anticipated."

"No," Luther shook his head. "Something is wrong."

"Want me to check it out, sir?" Owen came forward.

"Please," said the boss.

Owen was lifting his coat from a nearby hook when Luther paused him. "Stop down in the dining hall on your way out and fetch Alonzo to go with you. If Carmelo isn't where he's supposed to be, maybe his brother can be of some assistance in finding him."

"Very well, Mr. Irvin." Owen put on his coat and cap and went on his way.

~

I led Maude off the cliffs. We found a path that went uphill, bisected a stone wall, and continued back to The Hermann Hotel. I was relieved, right up until we passed Owen Topler walking with another one of Irvin's goons. They were heading for the ocean, surely about to look for the two men, only one of whom was supposed to be dead.

"Hiya, Roane." Owen tipped his cap to Maude. "Miss."

"Mornin', Owen," I said flatly.

Maude squeezed the blood from my hand as they passed behind us.

"They just saw us leaving the cliff walk," she said.

"So what?"

"We were the *only* people on it."

"Shit."

"Yeah," she said softly. "When we get back, get your things and come to my room. They're less likely to poke around there."

"Fine by me."

We hastened our pace. The hotel wasn't far.

# 14.

Owen and Alonzo traversed the cliff walk until they reached the tunnel's opening. The pair of mobsters looked around, seeing nothing.

"This is where Carmelo was supposed to burn Jay?" Alonzo asked.

"Yeah, yeah," Owen nodded. "I don't see nothin' and nobody, though."

"Knowing my, uh, unpredictable brother, he probably walked all the way into town to buy more cigarettes after he killed the fuckin' rat. He said he was runnin' low." Alonzo buttoned his coat to hold off the chilly breeze.

"He could be back in the hotel, for all we know," said Owen. "He's probably down in the speak as we speak."

"No, we would have passed him. One of the guys would have seen him."

"Maybe not. It's a big place." Owen turned back towards The Hermann. "Let's go back. He's down in the speak, I tell ya."

"He ain't at the hotel, Owen." Alonzo stared at the blood pooled on the rocks. "Looky over here."

"Looky at what? That's Jay's blood, obviously. Your peach of a brother did what he was supposed to do."

"Somethin' ain't right here." Alonzo dabbed a finger into the puddle of red.

"*You* ain't right... in the head. You're actin' loopy."

*I hope I am,* Alonzo thought. The gangster suppressed the fog of confusion and worry. He stood up, ready to turn around and follow Owen back to the hotel, when suddenly a gust of wind spat Carmelo's hat from the tunnel's throat. Alonzo's head swiveled. At first he thought it was an animal.

"Wait!" Alonzo called out.

"What?"

"That *hat*. That's my brother's."

"That's Carmelo's hat? How could he forget his hat all the way out here?"

"He didn't *forget* it." Alonzo picked up the hat and brushed it off. "He's here."

"Ain't nobody here, Alonzo."

"Shut up!" Alonzo walked to the edge of the cliff and looked down at the choppy waves, holding onto his own hat in fear that it, too, would be blown away.

He could see a man's leg bouncing up and down in the water. The rest of the corpse remained concealed by the cliffs. Leaning over any further for a better look would mean a sacrifice of balance.

"Someone's down there!" Alonzo exclaimed.

"It's probably Jay. A *dead* Jay," Owen shrugged.

Alonzo recognized the shoes and socks that matched his own.

"No, no! It's *not*. No!" He transformed into a maniac, pushed past Owen and quickly found a jagged, narrow crevasse that led to the beach. His brother's body floated in the shallow water, knocking against the rocks, trying like hell to be allowed into heaven. The icy water and loss of blood had already turned Carmelo as pale as parchment.

"No!" Alonzo cried out, followed by a hurricane of cursing in Italian, English, and then Italian again.

Owen followed and quickly realized the seriousness of what he was looking at. Jay's body was also there, floating nearby. Alonzo ran into the freezing ocean, the water up to his waist, tears sticking to his face. He clutched his cold, dead brother. Owen couldn't move, his heavy feet cemented in the wet sand.

∼

The staff at The Hermann was hurrying about, preparing for the Harvest Festival Ball set to take place later in the evening. I followed Maude through the main lobby of the Hotel and up the twisting crimson stairs. Her long legs jumped two steps at a time like a grasshopper. We passed only three people. Fortunately, none of them were Irvin's men. When we reached the second floor Maude turned to me.

"I'm in room 212," she said.

"You're on *this* floor? *They* are on *this* floor."

Maude gave me a puzzled look.

I continued, "Irvin and his people, Maude, are just down the hallway."

"Oh, I know that," she responded calmly. "That's the point, silly, they won't look right under their noses. Besides, I'm not in the registration log downstairs, so if they come poking around for *my* name they won't find anything."

"Not registered? *Why?*"

"I'll explain later, Emmett. Just do us both a favor right now and go get your things and get the hell back down here. Once we walk into my room and lock the door we aren't coming out until this blows over."

"I'm not gonna protest that."

"Yeah, well, hurry up. Get your cheeks back down here before I change my mind."

I made for the stairs without uttering another word.

"Room 212!" she shouted once more through the railing.

My feet were muted by the carpet as I ran down the hallway on the third floor. I unlocked my door and entered the room. There wasn't much to gather. I threw my clothing and bathroom supplies into the suitcase. The bottle of gin was still in the dresser drawer. I tossed it, along with the flask, into my suitcase.

~

Owen Topler, being the overgrown man that he was, carried Carmelo's very heavy and very wet body all the way back to the trunk of one of the gang's cars. Stopping only once to rest, he stayed off of paths the entire time to avoid running into anyone. The body, wrapped in their long coats, looked almost like a rug. Jay's body was simply left where it was because that's how rats were treated, floating between rocks at the mercy of fish.

Alonzo trailed behind Owen in a quiet state of shock. Occasionally he muttered something in Italian or kicked a helpless twig. He didn't care that his clothes were completely soaked in forty-degree weather, he didn't care about helping Owen carry the weight, he only cared about revenge. Revenge, he knew, would be hard to acquire now considering the man who apparently killed Carmelo had also perished. The only way at revenge would be to follow through with the mission that Jay wished to derail. Alonzo's blood was boiling.

The two mobsters entered The Hermann. Hames, manning the check-in desk, noticed the distraught men, one of them completely soaking wet and smelling like low tide. He stood. "Gentlemen, everything all right?"

"Fuck off," Alonzo yapped.

"All righty," Hames sat back down.

Owen and Alonzo thumped past room 212 and reached the series of rooms rented out by their boss. Inside the gang's temporary headquarters, the men were relaxing, playing cards and laughing. Alonzo's silent state of shock came to an abrupt end when he ripped the nearest lamp from the wall, hurled it to the other side of the room, and collapsed in a wail of unfiltered rage. From his knees, he began sobbing uncontrollably. The gangsters stopped enjoying themselves. Some of them reached for their guns; all of them tried to understand what was happening.

Luther burst into the room. "What the fucking hell is the problem here?" He looked at Alonzo and then up to the giant. "Owen, you wanna tell me what this shit is all about? You wanna draw the entire fucking hotel down on us?"

"Sir…" Owen said, standing over Alonzo's convulsing body.

"Somebody get him on the bed and shut him up!" Luther ordered.

Two men rushed over to Alonzo and threw him onto to the closest mattress, pinning him down and covering his mouth.

"Sir…" Owen looked at the rug and then to his boss. "We need to talk."

Behind the closed door of the boss's room, Owen told Luther and Wallace everything that was found on the cliffs and in the water. Luther listened from a plush chair as he took another small hit of opium.

"So you said you saw a bullet hole in Jay's head?" Luther pried.

"The back of his head, yes, sir." Owen held his bowler hat against his chest.

"And Carmelo was shot in the chest multiple times?"

"It appeared that way, yes, sir."

"Interesting," said Luther.

Wallace scratched his scalp with a pencil and crossed the room. "It doesn't take a tremendous brain to formulate what happened out on those rocks." His voice was staccato, like a typewriter. Luther and Owen both looked at Wallace, waiting on what he would say next. "There was a third party out there," Wallace proposed.

"Third party?" Owen looked befuddled.

"Third *person*," Wallace explained. "Carmelo executed Jay successfully." He walked behind Owen, his thumb and index finger aimed at the back of his head, mimicking a pistol.

"But..." said Luther.

Wallace went on, "Someone else showed up, felt threatened, and killed Carmelo."

"A monkey wrench in the process," Owen uttered.

"Exactly. A *big* monkey wrench." Wallace walked in front of Owen.

"A big fucking problem," said Luther.

The three men contemplated in quiet for a moment. Finally, Luther knew what to ask. "Owen, did you see anyone on the cliffs? Anyone else?"

"No, I don't think so."

Wallace dug further. "What about *near* the cliff walk? Was there anyone walking off of it?"

Owen admired the designs on the ceiling before returning his gaze to Wallace. "Yes, as a matter of fact, I *did.*"

"Can you describe what they looked like?" Wallace asked eagerly.

"How many people did you see?" Luther lisped.

"I saw two people, together, Emmett Roane and that blonde bearcat we met last night at dinner."

"You don't say," Wallace said slowly.

Luther rose from his chair. "That sandbagging son of a bitch."

"We can't be sure," said Wallace.

"Yeah, but we sure as hell can ask him some questions." Luther began pacing. "I wouldn't put it past Roane to try and play hero. I know the fucking type. Besides, we can't run the risk of him or the dame getting wise and trying to derail us like Jay did. Worst-case scenario is that Roane has one of those goddamn letters Jay wrote, spilling his guts about the plan for tomorrow. We can't risk not knowing."

"What are you proposing?" Wallace said.

"We *find* Roane and Goldilocks before they make a move I don't like."

Wallace put one of his hands up. "May I ask what move they could make that would be acceptable?"

"Dying," said Luther. The boss fixed his eyes up at Owen. "Take two men – *not* Alonzo – and go down to the front desk.

Ask that fruity fucking clerk what room Mr. Roane is staying in. Ask politely. When you find out what room, you bust in there, guns out, and take Roane by surprise. Try not to shoot him."

"You got it, sir."

"Good. Go. Do that *now*"

Owen hurried out of the room, snatched up two men, one of whom stuffed a Thompson under his trench coat. Alonzo lay still on the bed, a wreck, but slightly more controlled than during his lamp-throwing entrance.

The three mobsters tasked with apprehending Roane moved downstairs as if the steps were on fire. They approached Hames at a speed that bordered on a jog.

"May I help you, gentlemen?"

"I hope so, for your sake." Owen's voice slid over the desk like an avalanche. "I'm lookin' for an old friend of mine. Real swell guy by the name of Emmett Roane. Can you tell me what room he's staying in?"

"Oh, yes, yes, I know Mr. Roane. Give me a moment." Hames leafed through the registration book. "Mr. Roane is staying in room number 313."

"Thank you," said Owen. "Enjoy the party."

"You as well."

The trio hustled back up the stairs, this time past the second floor and to the third. They found room 313 and stood on either side of it. The gangster in the trench coat produced the Tommy gun, the other man a Colt 1911.

"Shall we knock?" one of them asked Owen.

"We're supposed to capture his ass by surprise, so no." Owen responded, pulling out his small revolver. "On me." The giant kicked the door in, splintering it at the latch. All three filed into the room, weapons extended.

Owen checked the bathroom, tearing the shower curtain from its rings. The man with the Thompson checked under the bed. The other man peeked into the closet only to find naked hangers. In room 313 the lights were on but nobody was home. Owen walked out of the bathroom and glanced at the other mobsters. The goon with the machine gun shook his head. "Ain't nothin' here but bed bugs, Owen."

~

Back on the second floor I stood in front of room 212 and knocked gently. I'm sure Romeo would have done the same. Maude cracked open the door, her cat-like eyes recognizing me in an instant. The door opened wide. She grabbed me around the collar and yanked me inside. Her lips pressed into mine with the force of a freight train behind them. Her hands slid down my shoulders, easing my muscles. Maude closed and locked the door behind me. She took a chair and jammed it up under the knob for additional security.

"I never..." I could hardly speak.

"Never what?" Maude said, her eyes level with mine.

"I never expected that. I was only gone for five minutes."

"It's a weekend of firsts, I'm sorry."

"Don't be." I dropped my suitcase and waited for her to say something. She didn't. She just gazed at the other side of the room. The space was much larger and more embellished than my room. I looked around and saw a huge bed with a veiled canopy, a claw-footed cast iron bathtub, a vanity fit for an entertainer, and a fancy liquor cabinet with a fat decanter.

Maude sat down on the edge of the bed and gave the wall the same look she gave the ocean earlier. The only difference was that the wall featured no whitecaps, no sound to answer her.

"I'm scared," she said, halfway between a breath and a voice.

"So am I."

"You don't act like it."

"Just because you can't see something doesn't mean it isn't there. I am scared." My hand slipped into my pocket, found the dead man's damaged paper, and uprooted it.

"Are you gonna show me what that is?"

"If you promise to remain calm."

"I will," she replied.

"This… this is why I'm scared," I said.

She took the paper from my fingers, unfolded it, and read it quietly. I watched as her eyes moved through the sentences uneasily. The handwriting was that of a nervous man trying to sound composed. The words were that of a dim man who used every shred of a meager mind to sound smart.

*"To the Frank Norelli,*

*I speaks as a nameless member of Luther Irvin's organisation, or what remains of it. As you know very well, Mr. Irvin's strength as a businessman has shrunk considerably in recent years and specially recent months. Before this weekend is over Mr. Irvin will have one lesser man on the count of me either running in the night or being killed for what I am about to share with you. I expose this because I can not, in good conscence, allow such an act of cowardise and terror to take place. It is my understanding that a young member of the Norelli family is to be married this Sunday in Newport. Mr. Irvin and those who agree with him are determined beyond a reasonable doubt to upset this occasion with violence. Luther Irvin has aquired a form of mustard gas and intends to use it on innocent lives attending the wedding reseption at Vanderbilt Hall. I bring this to your attention so that you can safe gaurd against Mr. Irvin's intended massacer.*

*I wish you the best of luck…. and a plenty of it."*

The letter wasn't signed. Its composer wasn't looking for credit, only prevention and probably a bit of internal redemption. As she read, Maude's mouth dropped open and her fingertips settled on her lips as the confession she held in her other hand began to seep into her heart. She stood up from the bed and walked away.

With her back to me she spoke. "My God. *This* is what they killed him for."

"For trying to do the right thing," I reinforced. "Irvin is a mad dog. He wants his seat back in the underworld and he'll go to any extreme to get it."

Maude turned back to me, a tear arching down her sharp face. "Emmett, a wedding reception for a Norelli – there'll be over three hundred people attending. Men… women… *children…* who have nothing to do with mobs or territory or bootlegging."

"I'm not gonna let that happen," I said, my voice hoarse.

Maude said, "The defector from Irvin's group, the one who wrote this, he intended to somehow give this to Frank Norelli *tonight* at the Harvest Festival Ball."

"I'm sorry – what?" I shifted in her direction. "Frank Norelli is coming *here? Tonight?"*

"Yes, I would be inclined to believe so. Anybody who is anybody in the area comes to the ball."

"So why the hell doesn't Irvin or one of his boys just plug Norelli here, tonight?"

"Because, Emmett, Luther Irvin wants *all* of the Norellis dead, not just Frank. He'll play it cool tonight."

I pressed my palm to the side of my head and then rubbed the bridge of my nose, oiling all the little moving parts of my mind.

"So, we stop this tonight."

"We stop this *now*. We bring this to the police," Maude suggested.

"Maude, the police aren't gonna believe it. Mustard gas hasn't existed for ten years. They'll laugh it off. I would have laughed it off, too, if I hadn't seen a man killed for it today."

"Two men," Maude reminded me.

"Yeah, two."

"So what do we do?"

I had only one logical resolution. "We go to this party tonight, we find Frank Norelli, and we give him that damn letter."

Maude contemplated for a moment. "We need to find you a tuxedo."

She stood, arms folded, with one hip poking out to the side. Her slight grin pointed upwards like a broken arrow.

"Just where the hell am I gonna find a tuxedo right now, Maude?"

"I have no idea, but you need one. This is a formal event, and without a tux you'll stick out like a sore thumb."

"So what am I supposed to do? Waltz on down to the local tailor, get all fitted up and buy one? I don't think so." I took one look at the phone on a nearby table and it came to me. "Can you reach the main desk on that phone?" I glanced up at Maude from the edge of the bed.

"Yes, why?"

"I may have an option. It's a complete shot in the dark but

what the hell."

"Well, I'm all ears."

"Dial the desk and hand me the phone, doll."

The phone rang only three times before he answered. "Front desk. This is Hames speaking. How may I be of service?"

"Hames, it's Emmett Roane."

"Mr. Roane!" His voice blew out my eardrum. "Are you enjoying your stay?"

"Yeah, it's really hitting all the sixes, Hames. Having a *swell* time."

"I see you have some friends here with you now."

"Friends?" *What the fuck was he talking about?*

"Yes, three men stopped at the desk a moment ago. A big guy said he was old friends with you."

I stared at Maude with eyes as wide and as cold as snowballs. The dots were connecting rapidly. Owen and that other thug had discovered the bodies and reported back to Luther. The boss was now sending "The Tank" and whoever else to find me. Maude and I were the only people seen around the cliff walk. We were now a priority for them.

"Ohh, yes." I spoke smoothly. "Old friends. Hey, ahh, Hames, I actually have a favor to ask."

"Anything, Mr. Roane."

"You wouldn't happen to have a spare tuxedo lying around anywhere would you?"

"A spare *tuxedo?*"

"Yeah, yeah. Or anything like it."

"As a matter of fact, Mr. Roane, you're in luck. I keep two tuxedos in the butler's pantry. Drinks and ash are so often spilled in this place that I've been forced to keep an extra around."

"You don't say…"

"I do say, sir. Are you in need of formal attire for this evening?"

"I actually am in need, Hames, if you don't mind… I figured we are close enough in size and you were my best bet."

"Not a problem, sir. I would be happy to lend it to you. Don't mind the stains on the outside, they're *hardly* noticeable. Don't mind the stains on the inside either."

"Wait, what?"

"Nothing, Mr. Roane, I'll be up momentarily to drop it off with you."

"Yeah, Hames, I'm actually residing in room 212 for the time being. If you could bring it to that room, I would much appreciate it."

"With pleasure, sir."

"And Hames, if anyone else asks what room I'm in, tell them that I'm still in 313.

"As you wish."

"Thank you, Hames."

"Expect a knock on 212 in five minutes."

I hung the receiver back on the phone and handed it to Maude.

"That sounded like it went well. Are you sure it's going to fit?" she said.

"Absolutely not."

Exactly five minutes after I got off the phone with Hames there was a knock on the door, sharp and fast like a woodpecker. I picked the .38 from my suitcase and cocked it. Maude unwedged the chair from the doorknob and pushed it to the side.

"Stand back," I said to her. I looked through the peephole and to my relief I could see Hames. I opened the door by about a foot, holding the gun behind my back.

"You're punctual," I told him.

"Most of the time," he replied. "You are staying with Miss Mable now?"

"Yeah, for now. Please keep this between us, bud."

"With the utmost discretion," said Hames as he handed me the tux.

"Thank you again for doing this."

"No sweat, Mr. Roane. Keep it."

"No, no, Hames… c'mon. I can't accept that."

"Yes, you can. It's old anyway. I have another."

"Thank you so much." I reached in my pocket, found my wallet and a ten-dollar bill inside of it. I offered him the money.

"You don't have to. Please don't," he refused.

"I *do* have to. Take this and get out of here."

He took the money and I added a smile. Hames smiled back and disappeared down the hall. I closed the door, locked it, and returned the chair back to its wedged position.

"Let me see that thing," Maude snatched the tux from me and

examined it.

"He offered it for free," I said.

"Yeah, because it's dreadful."

"Give me a break, lady."

"But it *is* a tuxedo, nonetheless. I doubt it will fit well. I can tell you're too broad."

I squinted at her with revulsion.

"I mean that in a *good* way. You have meat on you, which is a good thing, Emmett. Just not right now, when we need you to fit in this monkey suit."

"Jesus Christmas, Maude."

"It will be fine." She laughed. "We'll be fine."

Maude hooked the tuxedo onto the hat rack.

"We will be fine," she said again.

I prayed she was right.

# 15.

"How is Alonzo doing?" Owen asked Luther.

"He's been sitting up in bed and drinking heavily. I have two men sitting with him in case he decides to blow another gasket."

"I see."

Wallace adjusted his spectacles. "You're sure there was no one up there in Mr. Roane's room? No clues, nothing?"

"Nothin' but soap scum in the shower and dust on the rug. The other two boys will tell yus the same thing. Roane ain't up there."

"He's still here. I know it, just fucking *know* it," Luther said.

"Of course he's here," said Owen. "He's probably down in the speak right now having another drink with Goldilocks. I said that from the start. I'll go down there right now and break his neck."

"You definitely, most certainly, most positively will *not* be doing that. We've had enough trouble trying to kill someone discretely on the cliffs. What a joke. That is how we got into this mess. I should have picked out a better location to axe Jay in the first place. We need to stop drawing attention to ourselves."

"We can't just sit around and wait for the party," Owen said.

"That's *exactly* what we are going to do. You can go look in the speak if you want, Owen, but he isn't there. He's waiting."

"Waiting for what, boss?"

"Roane is waiting for the Harvest Festival Ball bullshit to begin, and when it does he'll slip down there with the dame and try and give Jay's letter to Frank Norelli." Luther stabbed a finger into the air. "*That's* what he's gonna try and do. That's what *Jay* was gonna try, I guarantee it."

Wallace said, "And just how do you plan on clipping Mr. Roane in the midst of a party with three hundred people in attendance?"

"I'll figure a way," Luther assured. "Whatever it is, they won't see it coming."

"Figure fast," said Wallace looking at his watch. "It's two o'clock now. Ball starts at seven. Five hours."

"More than enough time," Luther said. "I want everyone to rest up."

The boss turned and walked to the window. Gray skies still masked the sun. Darkness would fall fast.

"It's going to be a wild night, gentlemen."

~

Lined up next to the decanter in Maude's room were rocks glasses of various shapes and sizes. I held one of them up and admired the crystal. With light bouncing off it a certain way it was probably capable of signaling an S.O.S.

Maude smoked a cigarette while listening to the radio. She

152

was leaning on a table, gazing at me as if I was suddenly her prey. I put the crystal down and poured two fingers of gin into it.

"I'm not used to such nice things," I said to her.

"And I'm not used to such nice people."

"I'm not nice, Maude."

"You are."

"You saw me kill a man today."

"A bad man who would have killed us. You said it yourself."

"Maybe so, but that doesn't put me on the good list."

"Sure it does... you just don't know it yet," Maude urged.

I sipped the gin. Maude took one final drag of her cig before grinding it to death in an ashtray. Quickly, she walked over to me, snagged the glass from my hand and drained it. Another wave of heat rushed over me. Her perfume ate away at my brain like some potent narcotic. She poured herself another round, picked up a fresh glass and poured one for me.

"I would have made you one," I said.

"I could tell you were deep in thought."

"Oh yeah? About what?"

"About what happens next... in this room."

She was on target and I loved it.

"Why did you really come here, Maude? A woman isn't likely to be alone, especially one like you. "

"I came here looking for a piece of myself that broke off a long time ago," she said.

"What piece was that?"

"I won't know until I find it."

We drank and gazed at each other, trying to pierce each other's armor, trying to sneak a peek inside.

"What are you running from?" I asked.

Maude looked into my eyes before studying my scar more intently than she ever had.

"You want to know about my beauty mark." I poked the side of my head where it lay.

"You don't have to tell me," Maude said.

"The Great War. A great bullet licked me. I say *great* bullet because it mostly missed."

"You weren't always so pleased that it missed its mark," she said. "You weren't. You don't have to confirm it or deny it. I know."

I didn't nod, but the look I gave her played the part of one.

"You don't have to tell me how many men you killed before today either," she said.

"I won't." I looked at the wall and thanked her with a blink long enough to be considered a nap my some people. I hoped it would bounce off the walls and find its way between her ears.

"You lost someone, didn't you?" Maude asked.

"Don't we all?"

"Those of us who live long enough, yes."

"I did lose someone," I said. "Lost her the permanent way."

"I'm so sorry. How long since she passed?"

"A year and some days. When she slipped out of the world it was as though all the birds, everywhere, flew away with her. I see them flying, but I can't hear them. They may as well be on strings."

"I know all too well the feeling of being on strings," Maude said. "You think one thing and you're pulled the opposite way. You walk for miles with someone by your side, only to find out that you were walking backwards the entire time."

I realized then that Maude and I were more or less traveling on the same unpaved road, both of us finally walking forward.

"Anna would always wake up before me. Always."

"That was her name? Anna?"

"Yes." I nodded.

"What did you love most about her?"

I looked down at the rug and almost saw a female face in the designs. "Her sense of humor. I think some of it rubbed off on me. I hope it did."

"Go on," Maude said, her voice wringing a watery rag within me, one that had been heavy as hell for so long.

I said, "She would wake up very early and tell me about some wild dream she had, fall back asleep, and then ten minutes later wake up and tell me another dream, a new, wonderful story." I looked up from the rug and laughed a little. "One time she told me about a dream she had where half of my face was covered in moles and she had to bring me to the doctor."

Maude smiled. "Sounds like a nightmare."

"Not a nightmare, no," I said. "I know nightmares. On a good night I wake up and still hear her dreams in my ear. I'm just waiting to hear a story I haven't already heard."

"Maybe you'll wake up and be covered in moles," Maude said.

"Maybe, yes, if I'm lucky. More beauty marks." I gave her part of a smirk and a slight tilt of the head.

"You're the type that dreams of the past," Maude said.

"Don't we all?" I recycled the question.

"Some are afflicted more than others," she continued. "One third of the night's pie for me is the past, the next is the future, and the last third is a wild card."

"A wild card? I wish I had one of those handy."

"Last night I dreamt of this very moment," she said. "Do you believe that?"

"Does that count as the future or a wild card?"

"Both," Maude flashed her teeth at the declaration. I held her gaze and felt the large and lavish room shrinking with every twitch of her nose.

"Someday I'll have dreams where I don't see people that are gone," I said. "Maybe that's what the subconscious does. It brings you back so that you can try to put a period at the end of every sentence you remember them saying. They are kept alive somewhere in some swollen cavity behind your eyes so that if they return, for better or for worse, you'll be ready."

"If you spend enough time looking in life's rearview mirror you'll end up crashing into a light post," Maude said. She was studying me again. Not the scar this time, perhaps something underneath it. "I knew you before all of this."

"How do you mean?"

"A past life."

"A normal life?"

Maude laughed. "What's a normal life?"

"I wouldn't know."

"I wouldn't think you would."

"Why would I want the normal that other people have?" I asked both her and myself. "Go to the same place at the same time every day, punch in, sit down in some square space, and punch out? Sounds *riveting*. Thank you very much, but no thank you."

"You punch in and punch out now, do you not?" She made a point.

"Maybe so, but I only sit down in a square space on bad days," I replied.

"What do you think you were in your past life?" Maude asked.

"I don't know. I get the feeling I was a milkmaid."

"I'm being serious."

"So am I."

"Don't be foolish."

"I don't know, Maude. You seem to have all the answers. *You* tell *me*."

She leaned forward and flipped the transparent pages of a history book written about myself that I never read. "You were a gladiator in Rome."

"Nonsense," I said.

"A marvel of a gladiator. Yes, you were."

"You act like you're so sure."

"You were loved and feared and famous."

"And what were you? Some empress high up in the

Colosseum looking down on me?"

"I never looked down on you," Maude said with the confidence of someone who knew her memories well. She drank until she found her next question. "How do you feel about all of it? All of the violence in your life."

"In this life or the one spent in the Colosseum?"

"Either."

"It's never something that I go looking for. It looks for me and it typically finds its way." I drank.

"You make a living off of it."

"Because it's what I'm good at. I hate it, honestly."

"I know you do," Maude said.

I told her, "There are men of violence who wade through it because they must and because they can, then there are simply violent men. Luther Irvin is the latter of the two."

"It's like some souls get intoxicated by hurt," Maude said.

"Yeah," I said, "high off of hurt and God knows whatever else he puts into his body. He doesn't use violence to send a message or change things back into his favor. He likes it."

"You asked me what I'm running from," Maude said.

"I did."

"I'm running from a man who doesn't love me."

I gave her a questioning look. "A man?"

"My boyfriend," she said, washing the words down with alcohol.

"You... have someone?" I could feel my eyes wanting to leave my skull.

"He's a wealthy ass and a bully and a fool. I left him on Thursday night, stole some," she cleared her throat, "*more* than some of his money and drove out here to get the hell away. That's why my name isn't in the book downstairs... in case he comes looking for me. I figured they wouldn't miss me at my secretary job, so what the hell. I had to get away."

"Temporarily?"

"I don't know. I hope not," she said. The same tear I saw run down her face when we were on the cliffs resurfaced, as if starving for air.

"Some men are ugly. Some men are so ugly in so many ways," Maude said, her lips barely moving. I wiped the tear from her face and when I did her makeup smeared, revealing a concealed bruise around her right eye.

"*He* did this to you?"

"Yes," she whispered.

"If he was here now I *swear* I would – "

She threw herself against me and her arms wrapped around my neck as I grabbed her waist. Our lips locked, kissing long and deep. Her hands tunneled up the back of my shirt, pulling me closer.

"Is this what you want?" she asked in another whisper.

I answered by kissing her neck, her ear and her lips again, even harder than before. She pushed me towards the bed and ripped my shirt down the front. The buttons became another decoration on the rug. I flipped her onto the mattress and climbed on top of her, throwing my shirt to the floor. The rest of the world and all the weight attached to it evaporated. Everything I knew or ever wanted to know existed in that room, on that bed, without clothing.

We lay on an island temporary in time but buoyant and beautiful. Every time I closed my eyes and opened them again I could see it flourish. I breathed into her and felt the high, a high many people live a lifetime without experiencing.

I never wanted to let her go.

# 16.

Irvin's men were rising one by one, dressing and drinking in anticipation of the event downstairs. Aside from Luther, the only man who hadn't slept was Alonzo. The Italian sat in a chair tucked in the corner of one of the rooms, cleaning a Thompson without his brother beside him. He was eerily quiet, staring at the machine gun in his hands. Wallace had told him that his brother's killer wasn't Jay and wasn't dead – yet. And now, Alonzo knew about the real man responsible. Luther came into the room, sipping tea and dabbing his leaky lip.

"I can trust you to remain calm tonight, Alonzo?"

"Do I look calm to you?" Alonzo had transformed, over the past several hours, into a barely animated ice sculpture.

"When the time comes to kill Roane," Luther said, "we will seize it, but I can't allow any mistakes. Not again."

"When the time comes to kill Roane – *I'll* kill Roane." Alonzo raised his head. "I'll watch him die slowly. When I'm done with him, I'll cut up the blonde, too. Little pieces. Little piece like you give a baby."

"I'm sure something to that effect can be arranged." Luther sipped.

"Enjoy your tea, Mr. Irvin." Alonzo looked back down to the cold metal.

Luther strolled around the room, his voice growing louder as he spoke generally to his mobsters. "I want everyone ready to head downstairs at seven *sharp*. Nobody makes a move on Roane or the dame until *I* say so. If we fuck this up it's *over*. Try to enjoy yourselves or at least act like it, but not too much because, truly, I'm running *out* of patience."

"Sir," one of the men spoke. Luther turned.

"Mr. Irvin, what if Roane somehow makes it to Norelli before we can snag him?"

"He *won't,*" Luther insisted.

The boss finished his tea and placed the cup and saucer on a table near the radio.

"Nicky, where's the Clarinet?"

~

I don't know how long Maude and I made love for. Two hours, maybe three, before we eventually passed out. All I knew was that in that space and time there was no Luther Irvin, no Owen Topler, no dead men, no guns, no knives or mustard gas plot. There was no war, not the one I was in when I was eighteen and not the one I was in now. When I opened my eyes, it was night outside, a familiar friend that, for the first time in a long time, I didn't welcome. Maude lay in my arms, an angel. She was all I wanted or needed.

"What time is it?" Maude's voice was groggy.

I rolled over to the nightstand and found my watch. "Just after eight," I uttered.

"Party began an hour ago."

"We have to eat. I'm famished."

"What? You can't wait? I wore you out that bad?" She chuckled.

"Well, that's part of it, yeah. I'm just hungry as hell now. I haven't had a thing since before the cliff walk."

"Neither have I."

"I don't wanna waste time sitting down for a meal with both Irvin and Norelli prancing around the ballroom."

"Room service," Maude proposed.

"You have me sold." I lurched out of bed and shuffled to the phone completely bare-assed. When I dialed the main desk, someone other than Hames answered the phone. I figured he was probably putting on his other tuxedo and preparing for the ball. I requested that someone bring up a platter of various hors d'oeurvres and a bottle of champagne.

Maude propped herself up on a pillow, beaming at me through the blonde strands that fell to her eyes. The bed sheets barely covered her breasts.

"Now get back in this bed," she demanded.

The food arrived and we migrated to the floor. Maude and I sat there at the foot of the bed with the tray of appetizers between us, eating and sipping the champagne. She knew as well as I did that the meal, consisting of tiny delicious squares, might very well be our last, but neither one of us dared to admit it. I wore only my pants, my back against the dresser. Maude wrapped the bed sheet around her body like a toga and resembled a goddess more than ever. Her bruise was fully exposed near her right eye. It seemed to fade away right in front of me.

"How is your hand?" She looked at my makeshift bandage.

"It's fine, really. I've had a lot worse," I replied, knowing that before we ventured downstairs I would have to deal with it more thoroughly.

"What happens after tonight?" Maude asked.

"If we live, we have one hell of a story to tell."

"What will you do?"

I drank more champagne and gazed past Maude at nothing.

"I go back to Brooklyn, I suppose."

"Go back to flouncing around a boxing ring?"

"Maybe not; maybe I find something else. I've wanted to get out of fighting for a while anyway. It seems like it's all I've ever done."

Maude said, "We're always fighting, all of us, from the moment we are born and every day that we are lucky enough to wake up. That's all it ever really is. You only truly notice when you start losing."

"Well, you're not wrong," I said, looking into her eyes. I sipped more from the tall, slender glass. "What about you? What will you do?"

"I don't know," she said.

"Go back to *him?*"

"Not if I can help it."

"Run away with me," I said half-jokingly.

"I'll consider it," she said, bringing the champagne flute to her lower lip with an air of seriousness.

I checked my watch; it was getting close to nine.

"We have to get ready," I stood.

"Help me up," Maude raised both arms up to me. I held her hands and pulled her to her feet. The bed sheets began to slip down her chest. "Oops…" she muttered and caught it quickly.

"You plan on going to the party dressed like that?"

"Who's to stop me?" She gave me an eyebrow.

"Not me, I'll tell you that much." I kissed her and walked away. "I'll change in the bathroom. You'll have more room out here to put on whatever the hell you're going to put on."

"You'll hate it," she said.

"I somehow highly doubt that." I unhooked the tuxedo from the hat rack and swiped Maude's lighter from the table next to it.

In the bathroom, I made myself look a little less like a wild animal. It's amazing what some water and a bit of Dapper Dan can do. I removed the bandage from my left hand and pressed the sliced skin closed with Maude's tweezers. I then sparked the lighter and held the flame to the wound, cauterizing it closed. When the pain became unbearable I held my palm under cold running water. The wound was sealed, for now.

I held up the tuxedo – it wasn't the easiest thing on the eyes. It was tight and destined to rip, either between my shoulder blades or at the seat of my pants. I didn't a give a shit.

Once dressed, I lit a cigar and came out of the bathroom puffing the tobacco. The clock on the nightstand read twelve past nine. Maude was standing at the window with her back to me. She was putting on her second earing, using the reflection in the glass to fasten the jewelry. She noticed me step into the light and turned around; she was more resplendent than ever. Her gown was a tight black velvet that hugged her hips with diamond-like embroidering spiraling up the front. Her heels, headband, and matching bracelets all sparkled. Her dark red lips had returned, darker than ever and contrasting dramatically with the bright pearls around her neck. Those eyes, framed in shadow, hit me harder than any punch I had ever felt.

"Christ almighty…" was all I could manage.

I'm sure Christ Himself would have said the same.

"That bad, huh?" Maude said with a smirk.

"If by bad you mean ravishing, than yes."

"You can be charming when you want to be, Emmett Roane."

"It takes a lot to bring it out of me."

"Nice tux, by the way."

"Isn't it snazzy?" I pinched the collar.

"You'll impress all the ladies with that one."

"Will I? I was kinda only looking to woo one in particular."

Her smirk heightened into a smile, almost blinding me. "You already did woo that one, you dummy."

I blushed and told myself that it was the champagne. The truth was that she had me wrapped around her finger.

"You know that tux is gonna be totally destroyed before the night is over, right?"

"Don't say that. I'm growing into it, " I said.

"If those criminals don't rip it to shreds you can bet your buns that I will."

"I don't doubt it," I said as I tucked the .38 into my pants at the small of my back; its one bullet was better than none.

Maude walked to the dresser and picked up my flask. She looked at the engraving, running a finger over it. "I filled it up for you, the last of the gin." She tossed it to me.

I caught it. "Thanks, doll."

"You wanna go to a party?" She slid her tiny purse on one arm.

"Thought you'd never ask."

# 17.

Maude and I sailed down the hallway to the staircase arm in arm, the crimson carpet a river carrying us to our destination. We could hear the party roaring downstairs.

"E.S.R." Maude said. "Your initials on the flask."

"You're a bright bulb," I laughed.

"Shut up," she said with a playful slap to my arm. "I get the E and the R, but what is your middle name?"

"Shaun," I told her.

"Emmett Shaun Roane," my name rolled off her tongue as we descended the staircase further.

"And don't wear it out," I said. "What about you, Maude Mable? What middle name were you given?"

"Kathryn Nicole," she told me. "Kathryn with a y-n at the end instead of an i-n-e."

"Which one is it though? Kathryn or Nicole?"

"Both. My parents couldn't agree so they used both."

"Well, at least it has a nice ring to it."

"Thank you, good sir."

"My mother used to tell me that if I had been born a gal they would have named me *Penny.*"

"Dreadful," she said. "Doesn't fit you at all."

"Couldn't agree more."

The staircase twisted into the main lobby, revealing a crashing array of sights and sounds that roused the senses. The entrance to the ballroom was decorated with enormous pumpkins, squash and corn stalks hugging the pillars on either side. An immense banner hung high, strewn between the pillars, the writing on it a dark orange that read "Harvest Festival Ball," and below it, "Welcome." The steady noise of conversation, laughter, and clinking glasses rambled into the lobby. There had to be close to three hundred people celebrating.

"Now, *this* is a party," I said to Maude.

"Finding Norelli is going to be like finding a needle in a haystack," Maude said.

"Now is as good a time as ever to tell me what he looks like."

"Norelli has dark hair, kinda short in stature, Italian-looking. He'll be dressed nice."

"So basically he looks like everyone in here. Seriously, Maude?"

"I don't know, Emmett, he's hard to describe. I'll know him if I see him. They call him 'Buttsey' a lot on account of him smoking butts as if it's going out of style. So keep an ear open for 'Buttsey.'"

"I think I can manage that."

"As far as those blue eyes of yours are concerned, just keep a lookout for Irvin and his little boys. I'll worry about Norelli since I've seen his mug before."

"All right."

"And don't get yourself splifficated."

"Yes, madam."

"Don't call me *madam*, you wiseass."

A fair amount of the crowd loitered in the main lobby and outside the hotel's front steps. Maude and I took our place in a steadily moving line of new arrivals. The music grew louder with every approaching step. I could tell by the pace of the band that the event had already evolved well past the slower music and more conservative dancing. People were moving now, really moving.

Once at the ballroom's orifice, two men in tuxedos far better than the one I was wearing greeted us. One was a large man I had never seen before; the other was Hames.

"Invitation, sir," the larger man requested.

"They are O.K." Hames said to him. "Hotel guests and friends."

"Very good," said the other man. "Enjoy."

Hames shook my hand. "Fashionably late, Mr. Roane, Miss Mable."

"Wouldn't have it any other way," I replied.

"Speaking of fashionable, nice tux, Mr. Roane."

I smiled. "It's actually about to rip."

"Well, until then you'll look the part."

"Thanks to you, Hames."

He nodded. "Enjoy, sir... Miss Mable."

"We'll do our best," Maude said.

We passed under the banner and entered the ballroom. Instruments of all kinds piped, crashed, and boomed jazz over the ballroom. An attractive singer stood front and center, crooning into the microphone, hypnotizing the dance floor into a swinging frenzy. Round tables were set up similar to the previous night at dinner, except now only half of the people at them were sitting. Dinner was over and the only consumption for the rest of the night was to be almost exclusively alcohol. Dancing broke out and spread like wildfire throughout the entire ballroom, infecting partygoers beyond the dance floor and into the seating area. Glasses were spilled and broken. Confetti streamers hung from the ceiling while a thousand balloons, colored orange and silver, bounced over an intoxicated crowd. It was as if the speakeasy downstairs took over the ballroom and made it part of its tribe.

"I guess consumption and discretion aren't going hand in hand tonight," I said.

"The one night where prohibition doesn't exist," Maude replied. "Not here, anyway. You'll find off-duty cops, judges and lawyers partaking."

"It's like everyone is walking around in the same imagination," I said as I took it all in.

"That's one way of looking at it, yes." Maude tugged my tight sleeve.

I moved aimlessly with her through the raging scene, wondering what the hell was happening, and more importantly, how we would pinpoint Frank Norelli. A dozen flappers paraded by in a train of dazzlingly short, colorful dresses. Strings covering their attire swayed from side to side with the seductive movement of hips and exposed legs. Each woman wore a feathered headband. Above the feathers every flapper held up an oversized bottle of champagne with a small firework strapped to the bottle's neck, spewing sparks into the air. Maude caught me staring at them and tugged at my tux again.

"Focus, lover boy."

"We should have told room service to bring us one of *those.* "

She shot me one of her looks.

"I'm talking about the flaming bottles, Maude."

"*Sure* you are."

"Where do we start looking?"

"We go to the bar," she answered.

"Fine by me."

We looped back towards the makeshift bar area, which was near the entrance. To the side was a dumbwaiter that constantly ferried bottles up from the speakeasy below. The supply of booze appeared limitless. To someone with no knowledge of the dumbwaiter, it would likely appear as if bottles simply materialized.

"I doubt I'm even gonna need this flask tonight," I said.

"Ya never can know," Maude responded.

The bartender leaned forward. "What will it be, mister?"

"Southside for me," I ordered. "Manhattan for the lady."

"You got it," the bartender said and gave the order to a man behind him.

Maude ran her hand up my back. "You remembered my drink." She smiled.

"Of course," I said.

Maude kept a lookout for the mobsters while I paid the man. I handed her the Manhattan and we clinked our glasses together, sipped and looked around.

"I say we start back at the fireplace and snake our way, slow and wide, toward the dance floor. We're bound to find Norelli that way," I proposed.

"Yeah. We're also just as likely to stumble across the fellas we *don't* wanna find."

"Best defense is a good offense. If we find Irvin before he finds us, we can keep a watch on him. Dodge his moves better."

"Still thinking like a soldier, I see."

"Some things never go away. Lets get movin'."

The two of us drank as we bustled to the far end of the ballroom. A group of people gathered in front of a crackling fire. One woman sat on a man's lap, another woman whipped a broken corn stalk at a suitor trying to kiss her. All of them laughed hysterically. Maude and I carefully blended in. At this angle the ballroom seemed to carry on forever. The amount of people and confusion was, at the very least, intimidating.

"Needle in a haystack," Maude reminded me.

"Which is why we aren't wasting another minute."

I took her hand and steered us back into the fray. We weaved under streamers, slapped and kicked balloons out of our path, and cut between tables. When the traffic of partiers became too heavy, we would reroute slightly and keep moving, snaking and searching. I studied every face I could and watched every hand that suddenly disappeared inside a jacket. Each hand would come back out with a cigarette or a flask, never a gun.

A drunk approached Maude. "Hey baby, need a little lovin'?"

"No, thank you."

"Gal like you," he hiccupped, "needs somethin' nice."

"I got that earlier this evening," she pushed him away.

We kept going. As we picked up speed again I heard a loud, sharp pop next to us. I turned, my hand darting under my jacket and around the grip of the pistol. Maude clutched my free arm. Some dumbass was stepping on balloons, deliberately popping them. Another one burst, and then another.

"Jeeez," Maude gasped.

"Aaaand I just ripped my pants." I felt a breeze where I wasn't supposed to.

"Well, that was bound to happen."

"Is it bad?"

Maude looked at my backside. "No, it's not. Maybe big enough to fit a couple of fingers through," she said, "but that's all."

"Don't get any ideas."

Someone was approaching us from behind, someone in a hurry. I heard firm footsteps and felt the hairs on the back of my neck rise. I wheeled around, my hand still on the concealed .38. A girl stood before us with a tray of tiny glasses. She wore almost no clothing on her body, a smile on her face, and feathers on her head that peacocked high and wide.

"Shots of Mary Pickford?" She presented.

I exhaled audibly as a nervous tingling seeped out of my extremities.

"Why the hell not." I said and dropped a dollar onto the tray.

Maude and I drained the pineapple-flavored rum, named after the film actress, and placed the glasses back on the platter.

"Thank you, enjoy your night!" The gal said charmingly.

174

The shot girl walked away and when she did I wished she hadn't. Not because she was easy on the eyes, but because when she stepped aside, taking that tray and those feathers with her, I was staring directly at Luther Irvin. He and a cluster of his men were seated at a table. The only one I recognized other than Irvin was Wallace the worm. There were four of them altogether, all gazing out at the crowds of happy people, looking embittered. They didn't see us. I gave them my back and blocked them from spotting Maude.

"Do not move a single inch," I said to her.

"What? Why? Who do you see?"

"Irvin is seated at the table to my six o'clock. Twenty feet away. Look but *do not* stare."

She peaked. "Oh, hell."

"Yes," I said. "Oh hell. Now that we know where he is, we walk away nicey nice."

"Nicey nice, all right," Maude turned casually and we strolled away, each of us taking a long pull from our beverages.

Maude said, "Now we know where Frank Norelli is, too."

"How is that?"

"Would you be sitting anywhere even remotely close to your worst enemy? A man you hate? *No.* Which is why Norelli and his people are at the farthest possible table from where we were just standing."

"Over there?" I nodded to the corner of the ballroom farthest away.

"Near the dance floor," she said.

"Norelli likes to dance?"

"Probably not, but the crowd provides him with a blanket of

security. He knows that Irvin won't make an audacious move on him with so many witnesses around. He knows Irvin is desperate but not stupid."

"So he hides in plain sight."

"Precisely."

Maude and I broke from our snake pattern of canvassing the ballroom and began to head straight for the dance floor. Suddenly, I grabbed her. "Wait."

"What?"

"There were only four of them at Irvin's table," I said.

"How many were there last night?"

"I can't remember. Ten? Eleven? *More* than four, which means there are others up and about, probably combing the party for us. Owen definitely is; that bastard can see over everyone in here."

"And likely that little tubby squat, Nicky," Maude hypothesized.

"Just keep an eye out. These guys are playing for keeps."

Maude squeezed my hand. "So are we."

We pressed further into the party, dodging more balloons, flappers, and spillage. The dance floor was packed: men dancing with women, women dancing with women, moves of all sorts occupying the space. The sound of feet tapping on the floor and the band playing on the platform above made any words spoken more than three feet away imperceptible.

"I can't do that very well," I shouted to Maude.

"What?"

"I *can't* do *that* very *well!*"

"Can't do *what* very well?"

"*Dance*. I think I'm better with the slower songs!"

"Honey, there ain't gonna be any slow songs. Just move like I move and keep up with the tempo." She made it sound so simple.

"Seriously?"

"Yes, seriously," Maude responded. "And watch the perimeter for Frank Norelli. He has to be sitting nearby."

"I don't know what he looks like, Maude!"

"Then just dance, you fool! I'll look for him! You watch out for Irvin's boys!"

"I can't do this. I can't dance."

"With *me*, you can." She finished her drink and I finished mine.

Thank God for alcohol.

Maude grabbed my wrists and pulled me onto the dance floor. She moved expertly, rhythmically. She was exotic. I was not. I could already see men looking at her as she gyrated, most of them drooling.

"Maybe we shouldn't draw attention to ourselves, Maude!" I yelled over the music.

"Maybe you should get the lead out of your ass!"

I half expected her to say something like that. Maude performed the Charleston perfectly, drawing men to her like a moth to a flame. As they closed in on her I took her by the hand and spun her towards me, away from me, then to me again.

"Emmett! That's more like it!" Maude cheered. The tables and chairs along with the people seated at them came into view in fragments. From what I could see the area appeared mobsterless.

"Do you see anyone?" I hollered.

"No, not yet!"

I twirled her around again and pulled her to my chest. "How am I doing?"

"Surprisingly good. Must have been easy to get the lead out with that gap you have back there, heh?"

My lips pressed into hers, mashing the two smiles together and interrupting her laugh.

"We should split up," Maude said into my ear. "We can cover more of the floor."

"No, Maude! I'm not leaving you alo – "

"I'll be fine! If you lose me completely I'll find you at the bar in ten minutes."

"Fine," I said reluctantly. "Be careful!"

Maude danced her way into the jungle of vibrant headgear. The whirlpool of glad rags engulfed her. I heard a rather fanatical voice to my side.
"Well, look who it is!" *Shit*. I turned to see the flapper who had pinched my rear the previous night in the speakeasy. She and her friends moved at me like a pack of Amazons. They encircled my body, the leader finding the seat of my pants again, this time with a hole in it.

"Ohhh! Look at this!" She beamed. "Showed up ready for me this time, huh handsome?" *Oh no*.

They moved at me, licking their lips, preparing to devour me on the lambent floor. I danced with each of them one by one, twirling them away from me until I felt my manhood was safe. I could see people at tables more clearly now. To me, *every* man looked like Frank Norelli.

I scoured for Maude and witnessed a large empty circle forming in the crowd. From the wall of partygoers a midget emerged wearing a tuxedo, complete with a top hat, cane, and white shoes. The pint-sized man began tap-dancing with the ardency of four men twice his size, spinning his cane, clicking his feet, and pointing at the crowd. He flipped his top hat into the air and caught it on his head. Women around him flew in exuberance and picked him up, smothering him with hugs and kisses. This was officially the most bizarre party I had ever been to – and probably the greatest.

Maude stole back the attention of the crowd and continued dancing like Louise-goddamn-Brooks to such an extent that it began to make other women jealous. I'm fairly certain that if Maude had black hair instead of blonde she would have been mistaken for the dancer-actress. She rocked the Charleston once again, scanning the seating on her side of the dance floor as she moved.

Some lucky fella put his hand out for her to take, and she danced with him. Unfortunately for the sap, it didn't last long. Nicky appeared, cramming his heavy ball of a body between Maude and the man.

"Scusey me, pally." The gangster pushed the man away and stood in front of Maude, almost a foot shorter. "Miss Maude Mable. I almost forgot what a *dish* you are. Fancy seeing you shake a leg out here. Ya know... me and the fellas been lookin' for your gams all night. You and that boy-toy of yours, Emmett Roane."

"That so?"

"That is so." Nicky drank and grinned. "You wouldn't happen to have a piece of paper for me would yus?"

"I wouldn't know a thing about a paper," she responded serenely.

"I think you're a beauty of a liar, Miss Mable." Nicky produced a small automatic pistol from his inside pocket and discretely pressed it into Maude's stomach.

"I understand you're a blonde so I'll give it to yus real easy-like. You're gonna take a walk with me over to Mr. Irvin's table before I pop one up inside of ya... in the worst kinda way, missy."

The .38 was out of my waistband, the barrel pushed into Nicky's back. "The doll has more important things to do," I said. "Nicky, was it? I suggest you hand me that pea shooter, nicely."

"Mr. Roane... we was just talkin' about yus," he quivered.

"I won't ask again." I pushed the pistol into him harder.

"You're making a *big* mistake," he gritted and handed his gun to me.

Maude said to him, "Shouldn't you be greasing yourself up in some circus tent somewhere? Preparing yourself to be shot out of a cannon?"

"Take a hike!" I threw him off the dance floor so hard that he crashed into a cocktail cart and toppled over with it. With Nicky gone, Maude and I blended back into the crowd.

Her eyes locked on something or someone beyond my shoulder. "I'll be damned," Maude said.

"Please tell me something good," I tucked the .38 into my pants and dropped Nicky's tiny automatic into my pocket.

"Frank Norelli. He's here, standing at that table over there." She pointed with her nose. "White suit."

I turned around and found the man in white. He had dark hair, a big nose, and bags under his eyes that looked like sleepless half-moons. A woman sat to his right, likely his moll. The rest of the people around the table, I assumed, were his top men and their wives or girlfriends. He lived up to his name, "Buttsey", by lighting one end of a cigarette with the dying tip of another. I reached into my pocket and felt the letter.

"We have to act quickly," I said. "Nicky was the tip of the iceberg. He ain't the only one lookin' for us."

Maude interlaced her fingers with mine. We moved in full tilt in Frank Norelli's direction until we were close enough to hear complete sentences.

"But Franky," his moll moaned. "I just wanna dance."

"In a minute, baby." Norelli put a hand on her shoulder. "I'm just steppin' outside for a minute." He plucked the cig from his lips and bent over to kiss her. "Just gettin' some air, lovey." Norelli walked away from the table with two bodyguards, one in front of him, one behind him.

"He's heading for the back terrace," Maude said.

"Then we follow."

We scooted between tables until we were behind Norelli and his men. They walked along the ballroom's looming windows with Maude and me trailing at a distance.

Maude urged, "When we get out on that patio, we give him the letter. Irvin's men will likely stay in here, so it will be safer."

"Even if it isn't safer, we are getting this to him. *I* am getting this to him. Can't delay any longer."

Although the ballroom was enormous, there were only so many places to hide, and there was only so much room to dodge the enemy at a party that could very easily persist to dawn. The ballroom, in all of its glory, began to feel like a boxing ring, and the ropes were tightening around me.

Owen and another one of Irvin's men emerged from a nearby cluster of people and pivoted in our direction.

"Down! Down!" I yanked Maude behind a cloud of balloons. She peeked over the top and instantly saw what the problem was.

"Wait till they pass," I said. They probed around near our

cover for another fifteen seconds before moving on. I peered over the balloons and saw that the coast was clear. "They're gone, let's go!" I stood with Maude at my side.

"We're gonna lose him," she said.

Norelli was already at the end of the ballroom, crossing the fireplace. One of his men held the door to the terrace open for him.

"Take your heels off," I told Maude.

"Why?"

"Because we are running."

She held the straps of her footwear in one hand as we broke into a sprint down half of the ballroom, making a right turn at the fireplace and brushing past the more relaxed guests. Norelli was rapidly vanishing onto the back lawn. We opened the door to the patio, the cold air hitting us as if it were some errant epiphany, ruthless in the night. Our eyes panned the gatherings of people and conversations.

"I can't see him," I said, my voice on the edge of fear.

"I *can*." Maude pointed. "Next to the fountain."

Sure enough, Norelli was there, standing by the spraying water.

We navigated around one group of people and through another. The letter was now out of my pocket and in my free hand; every heartbeat drove me to rid myself of it. I envisioned the paper slipping from my fingers and into his. The burden was so close to being gone that I could already feel the weight lifting from my shoulders. Frank Norelli was close enough that I could smell his cigarette-soaked clothing when Maude pulled at my hand. Except it wasn't Maude pulling at me, it was someone pulling her.

Two of Irvin's goons had her by the arms.

"Em —" her scream was muffled by a hand.

"Maude!"

She was whisked from my grasp. I saw one of them jab something in her side. I struggled and felt what she must have felt: a needle. Two more gangsters, one of them Owen, materialized from the crowd and held my arms. Whatever injection they gave me coursed its way through my body with a sleepy vengeance.

"Hiya, Roane. You don't mind if I take this do ya?" The letter was his now.

My body was weakening, yet I felt oddly peaceful. I couldn't speak. I couldn't move. I could barely stand.

"I didn't think so," Owen snickered with his dumb smile.

Maude was guided away in the same haze as me. With my last centimeter of strength I looked back at Frank Norelli. He looked at me as though I was just another drunk unable to hold his liquor. I opened my mouth without words.

*I'm sorry, Frank.*

*I wish I could have.*

*I tried.*

I hammered against the walls of my mind, trying to find a way out. There was only blissful darkness.

# 18.

There's a funny thing about hospitals; the whiteness. The walls are white, usually the floors and ceilings are too, or almost white. The beds and pillows and curtains are white. Doctors and nurses typically dress in white. Patients wear white. Everything, everywhere is white and bright. It's almost as though they are preparing you for what may come next. If they can't fix you, and that other bright light decides to open up above, the transition from *here* to *there* won't be so hard. You just travel from one clean white space to another. The truth is – nothing is that easy, that simple.

It never is.

I'm in a hospital now, sitting in a chair with a window behind me. Rays of sunlight burn into the room, igniting the white tiles into a feverish glow. This is a memory that plays sloppily like an aged roll of film, except now it isn't sloppy or damaged. It is clear and bright and real. I have mailed this memory out in daydreams and nightmares. Each time I sent it away, I omitted a return address. Each time, it finds its way back to me.

I'm holding your hand, Anna, waiting for you to open your eyes. I listen to your breathing, wheezing, and coughing. You fight for air. I wish more than I have ever wished that I could give you my lungs. I wish that I could trade places with you, make you healthy again, give you back to the world – a world that needs more of your smile.

You smile now as you open your eyes. The room grows impossibly bright.

The pneumonia couldn't take that smile away from you.

"I thought you were gone," I say.

"I will be… soon," you whisper.

"Don't say that, Anna."

"We can't lie to ourselves, Emmett."

I grip your hand tighter while my free hand finds my face, holding in the pain.

"I'm not ready to lose you," I say. My own lungs feel like they are filling up now. It feels like I'm choking.

Each time you speak it's in an exhausted, yet peaceful, breath. It's as if you know of something good that I do not.

"How many times have I told you, Emmett? You will never *lose* me."

"Please…" Tears run between my fingers. I can hear them falling and crashing on the floor like drained hot air balloons.

"I am so proud of you. *My* tough guy."

"What do I do if I wake up –" I gasp for air; it feels like there is none in the room. "– If I wake up tomorrow and you aren't here anymore."

You run your finger over the scar on the side of my head.

"You live. You live your life. For both of us."

"I *can't,*" My voice cracks under pressure.

"You *can…* and you *will.*"

"No."

"Don't watch me. Let me go so I can watch you live. Watch *you* smile, for a change."

I never thought it possible to let out a laugh in the midst of tears, but I do at that moment.

"You're so beautiful," I say. "You're a great catch."

"I know I am… but what are you?"

We both laugh, somehow. You run your finger over my scar for the last time.

"Don't miss me," you say.

"How can I not?" I reply. We kiss between rays of light. The sun acts as a golden frame to us, a frame to a painted memory. A painting that is mostly white but is truthfully very many colors.

"I love you, Anna."

"I love you, Emmett. I'll see you someday, okay? Someday when you've done everything you ever wanted to do. Someday when you've held enough children and filled your life with enough laughter. Someday when I am but a memory buried beneath so many other good ones."

"Someday," I say.

"Until someday," you tell me.

Before you slip away from me, you say one more thing. One more thing that I could never understand.

Until now.

"Save them."

I will, Anna.

~

"Wake up, Mr. Roane." I heard a man's voice, and abruptly, my body was pulled tighter to the chair.

"I said, 'wake up.'"

I sat in a wooden chair, my feet tied to its legs, my hands roped behind my back. I fought the weight of my own head until my chin was finally off my chest. A solitary light bulb hung over me. It was bright; nothing else in the room was. I could see two men, no, three. There were shelves full of food and barrels likely full of booze. *A storage room,* I deduced. *Below The Hermann Hotel? Or some other building, town, or even state?*

The smell of opium lingered in front of me. His deformed mouth scowled.

"Rise and shine, pretty boy," he lisped.

My vision was still blurry and I could only definitively see him. The other men were merely apparitions. Luther inched closer and tapped me on the top of the head with something hard, maybe the barrel of a gun or the end of a pipe.

"Wakey-wakey," the ghoul said. "Rise and shine."

All I could do was groan. More and more of the picture came into view. My tuxedo tie was gone. The white shirt was ripped open at the top and stained with blood. My lip had been bleeding; I tasted the metallic flavor. One of the cowards probably hit me while I was unconscious. I still had my tuxedo jacket on. Miraculously, I could feel the flask still hiding in the left inside pocket.

Not surprisingly the back of the jacket was now ripped in accordance with my pants. Luther tapped me on the head again with what I could now distinguish as a piece of an opium pipe. "Had a nice nap, did we?" He pulled up a stool, sat down in front of me, and began to assemble the smoking apparatus. "You've slept well. Do you know what day it is?" he asked.

"Not really."

"It's Sunday. Very shortly I have a wedding reception to attend. Going to be a real swell time, maybe even more so than last night."

"Fabulous."

"Do you like my pipe? I call it the Clarinet."

"How very creative of you."

"I call my car the Kettle." he smiled. "I call it that because that was the only toy I had as a child. I used to bang on it with spoons and make music when my mother wasn't home. When I was tired of music I would boil me some water in that kettle she loved so much. The water would get too hot to touch and I would pour it on the dog as he slept. I would listen to him cry as it burned. Burn, *burn*, burn."

"Again, very creative."

"I had my men give you a real happy shot before; the girl, too. Just a little morphine… well, a lot of morphine. I use it myself when I run out of this here Chinese molasses. I gave you a *concentrated* dose. Made it easy for us to scoot you and Miss Mable out of the party like a couple of over-served children." Luther packed the pipe with opium.

I struggled to speak. "Where is she?"

"The girl? Oh, she's safe, for now. Not far from here."

"Why am I still alive?"

"Because we have been forced to wait for a safe place and time to deprive you of your existence. A lot of happy people were at that party. Some of them still here, even with the sun bleeding into this omnipotent place. Wouldn't want to have ruined their good time now, would we?"

"I'm in the basement of The Hermann, is that it? In some big closet?"

"How very perceptive you are, Mr. Roane. Remarkable, considering the amount of times you've been smacked around in your worthless fucking life." Luther lit the opium and inhaled. He blew the smoke in my face and laughed. "Would you like a puff, Mr. Roane? May be the last opportunity you ever have."

"Take your pipe and shove it up your ass." I looked at the gangster near the door holding a Winchester shotgun. "Better yet, shove it up *his* ass."

The gangster racked the pump on the trench gun. "You better watch your fucking mouth, mister!"

"Did you pose in front of the mirror all night holding that cannon thinking you look tough?" I asked. "You still look like a whore's beaver to me."

"Hey, fuck you!" the gangster exploded.

"Easy now!" Luther shouted. "No need for the tension. Mr. Roane is all talk, see. Ropes are nice and snug. All he has is that stupid mouth of his."

"Prettier than yours, clown."

"Well... you aren't wrong about that." Luther said before sparking the drug again.

Smoke drifted around the room like confused thoughts lost between men. "You know, Mr. Roane here is really quite an interesting fellow. Before becoming a 'butcher' in the boxing ring, old Emmett here was something of a war hero against the Huns. That's right, a bit of a legend. Rumor has it that a flock of doughboys were being cut to ribbons by two pillboxes. Emmett finally had enough, so he climbed out of the mud and took both them pillboxes out himself. Saved a lot of lives. A real *hero*.

Then, when they wanted to award him a medal, he tried to refuse. Icing on the cake. Real *selfless*."

I stared into his hateful eyes, saying nothing.

"As you can see, gentlemen, Mr. Roane has a real tendency for theatrics, which explains why he tried like the dickens to get in our way. I also find it wildly ironic that we'll be using mustard gas to assist in our, um, massacring of the Norelli family." Luther puffed the opium. "Oh... and by family, I mean *entire* family."

"You're a monster," I said through tightening teeth.

"You remember mustard gas from the trenches, don't you, Emmett?"

"How did you get it?"

"I didn't get it, I made it. Not a lot, but what I have kills a lot faster than the elementary shit you saw in Europe. I made it extra potent, just like life itself."

His men laughed along with him. My hands strained against the ropes; Luther was right, they were very snug.

He went on, "We simply toss a few canisters into that wedding reception, seal the doors, and machine gun anyone lucky enough to get out. It's a shame, really. I love weddings."

"You won't," I growled.

"I rather think I will, dear boy."

"I'll be between you and those people, even if I have to crawl there."

"There you go with the hero thing again. Old habits die hard, I guess. At least you're optimistic. You know, I fought in the war, too, Mr. Roane. Except I wasn't a hero. No, no, no. I was just a young man who got his face ruined when a fucking grenade exploded on my friend, taking my lip to hell in the

190

process."

"You'll be joining your lip soon enough," I promised him.

"You really think you can stop me? Allow me to save you the trouble by telling you that it isn't *worth* stopping me. This will go on forever, all over the country. It will only stop when Prohibition ends, and Prohibition *won't* end. The righteous people of this country will make sure it won't end. Mobs are going to be killing mobs, blood is going to keep being spilled. The only ones who get to the top and *stay* on top are the ones, like me, who are willing to accept living in a world devoid of rules. No morality, no omerta bullshit, no family. Only a business. A fire that you feed."

"Better go feed it then, Luther."

"Ohh, I intend to." He disassembled the pipe and placed it in a clarinet case. "I tell ya what, Emmett. I feel quite *chipper* right now."

"I'm so glad," I said flatly. "Don't let the door hit you on the way out."

"Such a vibrant sense of humor. Such a waste. You act like it's fun but it can't possibly be any fun behaving like some stubborn village idiot altruist. Underneath your coarse exterior you're nothing but a stick of butter awaiting a hot knife. Your fucking morals did you good, huh? Got you in the hot seat you're presently in."

"I'd rather be an altruist than a sadist, or worse, an egoist," I responded.

"You really don't see the bigger picture, Mr. Roane."

"Wiping out a wedding – "

"A wedding reception," he corrected me.

"Wiping out a wedding reception won't bring you any closer to your past, Mr. Irvin."

"I'm not talking about today's plans," he said. "I'm talking about much more. I'm fascinated by ancient Rome. Are you familiar?"

I felt bumps rise on my skin before I could answer. "Yes."

"I've got it all figured out." Luther's bloodshot eyes stretched. "You're Mars, god of war, spring and justice. Patron of the legions and divine father of Romulus and Remus. Or are you Janus? Yes," he said with a hiss. "Janus, god of new beginnings, endings, transitions, doorways, keys. I see you as the latter. Having said all that, I regret to inform you that you will find no key out of here, no beginning. Only a locked door behind locked doors and an ending. The transition will be from here to whatever hell you believe in… or just blackness… probably blackness."

"Stop talking," I said. "It's annoying and I have a headache. Shut up."

"You shut up, Roane. See now, I've studied gods in all forms, even more than I've studied chemistry. I've searched for meaning and such."

"I have a theory," I said.

"Yes?"

"You talked your lip to death. It just fucked off a while back because it didn't wanna work anymore."

Luther shook his head and ignored me. "I assure you that there are no deities beyond the barriers of our minds. That's what makes all of us gods: you, me. Miss Mable may be Venus for all we know."

"Who are you supposed to be, then?" I asked. "Lemures?"

He loved it. "God of the malevolent dead. Very good, Mr. Roane, very good. Lemures, leader of the wandering and the vengeful. I and my restless manes, left here to torment and terrify the living."

"Poetic," I said.

"Only justice is poetic."

"You bet your sweet ass it is." I winked.

Luther stood from his stool and reached into his jacket. He pulled out my .38 and held it between us. "I was always fond of these Smith & Wesson's. You don't mind if I borrow this, do you?"

"Knock yourself out, Luther."

"Why, thank you, kind sir." He slipped it back inside his suit.

"Welcome."

"Oh, and Emmett... you should have used the lonely bullet housed in this thing on yourself. Could have saved us all a *lot* of trouble."

I glared at him as he opened the door halfway.

"I'll be leaving you here with Alonzo. I hope you don't mind. You killed his brother on the cliff walk so he asked me if he could have a word with you. He's really an artist by nature. His surname is Pelaratto, which in a sense means *rat peeler*. Fitting. Unfortunate that he's the only peeler of rats I have left. I watched him slice a man's nose clean off in one swipe a couple of weeks ago."

"Good," I said. "Mine has been itchin' something awful lately."

"Such a sport you are. Bye, Mr. Roane."

"See ya around, Mr. Irvin."

The door slammed behind him.

# 19.

I looked at the man standing at the door, who looked at the man standing in the dark. Out of reach from the solitary bulb's light, the man whose brother I shot off the cliff lit a cigarette. The flame unsheltered his face. For a moment, I thought I was staring at the same man I watched die.

The cigarette's amber glowed in the way a faulty lighthouse would, beckoning a ship to an imminent end. The mobster stepped into the light and the shadow cast by his hat left only the bottom half of his face for me to see.

"I knew you was gonna be a problem the moment you walked over and sat at the boss's table the other night," he said.

"I tend to rub some people the wrong way, men mostly," I informed him. "I rub women the right way. Usually."

"And now my brother, my own flesh and blood, is dead... because of you, you fuckin' Irish pig."

"I'm half Italian." I thought maybe that would obtain me some points.

"Not to me, you aint."

It didn't.

The mobster unsheathed a stiletto knife that was identical to the one his brother pulled on the cliff. He ran his finger down the edge of the blade. "Lucky for you, I sharpened it today."

"Praise Jesus."

"Unlucky for you, I intend to take my time… cut off the little pieces first and show 'em to yus."

"You can leave my lucky sausage where it is. I can see it fine. Well, not right now, obviously, because my pants are still on… but you get the idea."

"Ha-ha-ha," he bellowed a fake laugh. "You really missed your calling as a fuckin' comedian."

"I sorta like what I do," I said.

"Like what? Being an average boxer?"

"No. Killing assholes."

His eyes flared with a twitch of his lips. "I think I've heard just about enough shit come out of your trap!" He came close enough for me to smell onions on his breath.

I flexed as hard as I could against the ropes. It was no use. There was no way out. My brain had already begun to find ways to accept a horrible death. Not just my own demise but Maude's and countless others. I was at the end of everything when I felt something: a square shape in one of my back pockets. I moved my fingers towards it.

"The Butcher of Brooklyn,' heh? I think it's time 'The Butcher' got butchered." He put the knife to the top of my nose. "Think I'll cut this from your face. That way you won't be able to sniff around in other people's business ever again."

My fingertips pinched the corner of what was in my back pocket. A box of matches.

"Wait!" I yelled.

Alonzo took the knife away from my nose. "Why Emmett Roane… I didn't take you for the pleading type."

"I'm not. I just want a smoke before you do whatever the fuck you intend to do. There's a stump of a cigar in my right inside pocket. Please."

Behind me, I worked my fingers towards the matches. The gangsters glanced at each other with eyebrows raised.

"Just one last smoke," I said.

"Fine," said Alonzo.

"My right inside pocket. Thank you."

Alonzo reached into my jacket and found the cigar. "This fuckin' turd what you're talkin' about?"

"Yes," I answered.

He pushed the soggy end of the cigar between my lips. I clamped down on it nervously. Behind me the box of matches was almost completely out of my pocket.

"Got a light?" I asked.

"Certainly," he said. He flipped open a lighter and leaned forward, smiling behind the flame, moving it from side to side facetiously before finally lighting the cigar.

As he straightened himself I noticed a Colt 1911 sticking out from the front of his pants. The dummy had it cocked with the safety off. I puffed the cigar like it was my last, which was a distinct possibility. The smoke filled the area around my chair.

My roped hands slid a match from the box.

"Roane, ya ever heard the joke about the Irish guy with no legs?" Alonzo asked.

"I haven't."

"It goes something like this…"

I struck the match against the ignition strip, evidently not hard enough.

"So this mick is hangin' out on the beach with no legs, all by his self, and three dames come walkin' on by."

I struck the match again and felt the spark die under my thumb.

"The first dame walks over to him. She bends down and asks the fella if he's ever been hugged. The mick says, 'no, no, I've never been hugged.'"

He rambled on and I struck the match a third time. A flame breathed to life and I held the match to the ropes. All the while the cigar smoke masked the burning twine and blistering smell.

"So the dame bends down and gives him a kiss. The mick says, 'thank you, thank you.' The third dame walks up and asks the mick – "

"Wait," I interrupted, my teeth still clenched on the cigar, holding back the pain of the tiny inferno behind me. Freedom always comes with a price.

"What now, Roane?" He retorted angrily.

"I think I've heard this joke before. The one about the tide coming in, am I right?"

"Yeah. Damn."

"Well, I have a joke of my own, two jokes to be exact."

"Oh yeah, comedian? Make it fast."

"The first one is that your boss was wrong. It wasn't two pillboxes I took out, it was three…"

"Yeah? Big deal."

"The second one," I said and spat out the smoldering cigar, "is that you're both *fucked.*"

My hands flew out from behind me like some winged hellhound, flinging flaming rope in both directions. In one move, I pulled the pistol from Alonzo's pants and shot him through the bottom of his chin. The bullet exited the top of his head and popped his hat off like a champagne cork. To my right, the gangster by the door raised the shotgun. My mind moved in slow motion. I kicked myself backwards as a shotgun blast narrowly missed my head, the pellets shattering into the cement wall to my left. From my back, I put two rounds into the mobster's chest. He stumbled back to the wall and slid down it. I put the smoking barrel of the 1911 to the ropes between my legs and squeezed the trigger again, severing the ties completely. My body scrambled out of the restrictions.

I kicked the chair away from me and stood but fell back to the floor; my legs were asleep. I flipped the safety on the Colt before shoving it in to my waistband. I reached for the dead mobster's Winchester, and with one hand on the barrel and another on the wall, I was able to lift myself up. I leaned against the wall, allowing my legs to awaken. The Winchester's pump slid back and forth under my palm, ejecting the shell that nearly took my head off and chambering a fresh one. *I need to find Maude.*

I opened the storage room door cautiously and poked my head into the tight corridor. The hallway on either side of me was clear. I heard voices to the right and decided to proceed in that direction. With the shotgun extended in front of me I walked at an audacious pace towards the sound. After what felt like the length of a city block, I made a ninety-degree turn into another long thin hall. A cook stepped out of the kitchen and blocked my line of sight.

"Get back in there, now!" I commanded. "Stay out of the hallway!"

The cook disappeared.

At the end of the corridor, another one of Irvin's men stood sentry in front of a door near the service elevator. He saw me and shouted something I couldn't understand. His pistol glinted in a nearby light as he aimed it at me and fired twice. The rounds skipped off the wall to my right. I continued moving at him and unleashed a spread from the trench gun. Shotgun pellets blanketed the left side of his body, knocking him into the wall but not having enough vigor at such a range to kill. He fired two more times at me; a bullet whizzed over my head and another chipped the wall to my left.

"Emmett!" It was Maude's voice. "Help!"

The cry was coming from inside the room the gangster had been guarding. I was close enough to him now, so I pumped and fired again. The blast hit him directly and put him on his ass.

"Emmett!" Maude screamed from the other side of the door.

I tried the knob. Locked.

I racked another shell into the trench gun and lowered the barrel to the lock. The concussion blew the latch and everything around it to pieces. I booted the door open and saw a mobster standing next to a terrified Maude, who was tied to a chair and trembling. The goon held a Thompson to her head. I pumped the shotgun once more and pointed it at his upper chest. He tried to sound brawny. I almost felt bad for him.

"Make another move, Roane, and I'll cut the broad in ha – " I cut his sentence and practically his body in half, dispatching him into a back flip. I let go of the shotgun and it clattered to the floor.

My ears were ringing so badly that I could barely hear a fucking thing. I picked up the Tommy gun and checked that it was ready to fire by removing the fifty-round drum magazine and eyeing the bullets inside. I clicked the drum back into place. The top bolt was already pulled back and the safety was off.

Maude's mouth was moving, but invisible bells prevented me

from understanding what she was telling me. The wound on my left palm had opened up again in the action, and blood ran down my wrist. Both wrists were burned slightly pink from my escape.

I looked around to see a storage room similar to the one I had broken out of. She was nodding at a table in front of her. There was an ashtray and a knife beside it. That's what she was saying: "*knife.*"

I hurried to the table and picked it up, knocking the ashtray to the floor. I knelt down in front of her and shaved the ropes from her body.

"Thank you!" she said.

Sound was returning, unfortunately at full volume. "Thank you!" Maude said. She was sweating, her mascara running, her lipstick smeared. Her dress had been ripped, and her pearls were missing.

"Did they hurt you?" I asked.

Maude fought off the sliced ropes as if they were poisonous snakes.

"Did they hurt you?" I repeated

"No! No, I don't think so. Not really."

"You're all right?" I checked her over.

"Yes, yes. I've had much worse than these blockheads."

I remembered what Maude had revealed to me about her boyfriend.

She stood from the chair. "What the hell is happening?"

"They stuck us both with morphine and threw us down here. We're in the basement. They're out there moving the mustard gas. I got out and killed four of them. More of them are gonna be down here, though, I promise you that, so we have to move. The entire hotel probably heard shooting."

"Christ, what are we gonna do?" Maude frantically rubbed the rope marks on her wrists.

"I need you to get upstairs and get to a phone. Stay *out* of sight. Get to a phone and call the police."

"*Now* you want to call the police?"

I checked the gangster's body for more Thompson ammo and found an additional stick magazine.

"We don't have much of a choice. Tell them there are heavily armed men preparing a hit on Vanderbilt Hall. Tell them that gunfire has been exchanged at The Hermann Hotel. When you've done that, get to your car and get it running."

"What are you gonna do?"

"Everything I can," I said and kissed her as if it was the last kiss I would ever give – another distinct possibility.

I pulled her out of the storage room and pointed the Tommy gun down the long corridor.

"Take the service elevator to the third floor; they are less likely to be up there. Get to a room and to a phone."

"Okay, okay!"

"When you press the button for the third floor, hold down the button. It should bypass the other floors and get you there quicker. You'll be less likely to bump into one of them that way."

We moved closer to the elevator and I hit the call button with the barrel of the Thompson. I glanced at the dead gangster sprawled out in the hallway and noticed another small handgun poking out of his coat. I handed it to Maude. "Take this just in case. Do you know how to use it?"

"I've been to a range… once," she responded hesitantly.

"Pull the slide back." I watched her do it. "Good, now if you need to, just point and squeeze."

"Easy for you," she said.

I opened the gate and Maude entered the elevator. Her thumb pushed down on the third floor button and she held it there.

"Which way are you going?" she asked.

"I'll take the back stairs, hook around the outside of the hotel and ambush them." I secured the gate and was watching the elevator doors close when Maude, at the last second, caught sight of something over my shoulder and screamed.

"Behind you, Emmett!"

I turned around. Owen Topler's massive frame eclipsed the light halfway down the corridor. He aimed his tiny revolver at me.

"Hiya, Roane."

He fired all six of his bullets wildly. His aim was poor but not poor enough to miss me completely. Before I could raise the Thompson, one of his rounds found its way to my chest and knocked me to the floor, pushing the wind from my lungs as I fell backwards. From my back I could see one of the ceiling lamps swinging, mocking a referee's arm; it, too, had been struck by a bullet. There was a hole in my jacket somewhere near my heart accompanied by a warm liquid leaking out. The pain was intense.

I raised my head and looked down the hallway. From between my feet I could see Owen strolling towards my flattened body. The small revolver was dwarfed by his humongous hands; its cylinder open, spent shells falling to the floor with a jingle. The Tommy gun, flung from my grasp, lay well past my feet and out of reach.

"Roane, Roane, Roane," Owen rang out while reloading. "Always making things so damn difficult for yourself. Always taking the high road. Can't except defeat. Not in the boxing ring and apparently not in *life* either."

I felt around the front of my belt for the Colt 1911 and realized that it had also been displaced by the impact of Owen's bullet. *Owen's bullet... where had it hit me exactly? The pain was intense before, but why had it stopped now? Why was my shirt not dyed red? How was I still breathing?* My hands began to palpate from my waist and up my torso. The tuxedo was soaked. I smelled the substance on my hand and tasted it. I was bleeding gin.

The round had penetrated one side of the stainless steel flask but only managed to dent the back of it. Owen successfully assassinated my favorite canteen but failed to murder me.

The Tank was fully loaded again and grinning. "Why can't you just die like a fuckin' dog? You have to go and be selfish, taking others with you. My *friends*." He hovered over me, cocked the hammer of his pistol and aimed it at my face. "What was it you used to always say on the canvas, Roane? In the heat of a fight you would always say it. When you was really gettin' rattled and angry. I used to get a real kick out of it. What was it?"

My body shifted slightly and I could feel the 1911 under my back. I looked at the trigger guard of the revolver he had pointed at me.

"Don't miss me," I snarled.

With the index finger of my left hand I filled the void behind his gun's trigger, preventing it from compressing and ending my life. Owen squeezed with all his might. The trigger was crushing my finger, but it was unable to move back far enough to fire. I gripped the Colt beneath me with my right hand, flicked the safety off, and hoisted the barrel to Owen's leg. He caught the 1911 by the slide and pushed back. I pulled the trigger and the bullet cut into Owen's thigh. It's recoil sent the Colt catapulting from both of our hands. It bounced somewhere behind me near the elevator.

Owen clutched his leg, howled and stumbled back. I punted the giant in the groin and used both hands to fight for control of his revolver. Back on my feet, I pried the pistol from him, slamming his body into the wall with my own. He came around with a haymaker that banged into the side of my face. My balance was gone, taking Owen's pistol with it and sending it tumbling towards the other end of the hallway. Now we were both unarmed.

He transformed into a raging bull. With brute strength he grabbed hold of my tuxedo jacket's collar and flung me through a door. A closed door. I landed in the kitchen, surrounded by pieces of splintered wood. The Tank stepped through the hole he had made with my body. At the sight of this, the only cook remaining in the kitchen decided to take the rest of the day off.

I propped myself up on my elbows and shook my head in an effort to collect my senses. He was already standing over me.

"You know, this isn't for sport this time," Owen said. "This is me killing you."

Owen latched onto my jacket and lifted me from the floor. The rip on the back of my coat expanded under my own weight, shredding the tux completely and sending me spinning to the floor like a falling ball of yarn. I dropped hard again on the kitchen tiles. Owen held a piece of the ripped black cloth and looked at me heatedly. I kicked the wound on his leg, sending him howling again and using the diversion to pick myself up.

My fists attacked his ribs and face in a string of rapid jabs that took him by surprise. He regained his defenses and punched me twice, once high and once low. I ducked his third swing and came back at him with another assault. My blows, while moderately effective, angered him more than anything else.

I doubled over from a shot he connected with my stomach. While I struggled to find my breath, he grabbed me around the neck and launched me over a preparation counter. I tumbled through pots, pans, plates, and food, most of it crashing to the floor with me on the other side. The Tank surged around the corner and swiped a butcher's knife from the counter. I clambered to my feet and readied myself for combat. In my right hand I gripped a potato peeler.

Owen laughed. "Funny that you die with a potato peeler in your paw, you fuckin' leprechaun."

I threw it at him as hard as I could. The blade lodged itself in one of his thick pectoral muscles. Owen looked down at the protruding peeler.

"Really?" he said.

I shrugged back.

Owen pulled the potato peeler from his chest and charged at me. I dodged the thick knife several times, finally deflecting it with a frying pan. I wound up and belted Owen in the head with the pan hard enough for the handle to snap. It did very little.

"Dammit!" I cursed.

The big boy came at me again, the knife heading directly for my eye. I caught his hands with mine and stopped the blade a quarter of an inch from my pupil. As we wrestled, my back banged into the stove. Behind my head a large pot of boiling water caused my neck to perspire. The butcher's knife cut into my eyebrow, drawing blood. I would either be skewered or boiled. Perhaps both, turning me into a kabob of some sort.

I jerked to the side, which caused Owen's knife hand to dive into the scalding hot water. I grabbed his arm and held it there for three long seconds as he screamed in raw agony. When he finally freed his arm from the pot, the skin from his elbow down had been badly burned to a bubbly red. Owen dropped the long knife to the floor and stared at his boiled limb as though it was no longer his own.

"What... *What* did you do to me?"

"You're not completely unlike me, Owen." I picked up the steaming knife. "Someone tells you a stove is hot, and you're stupid enough to go and touch it anyway."

I stabbed him through the heart and twisted.

For Owen "The Tank" Topler, the party was over.

~

In front of The Hermann Hotel, Luther Irvin had the gang's fleet of three cars assembled. Two 1924 Chrysler Model B-70s, one brown and one tan, were parked side by side in the driveway. Luther's salmon-colored Studebaker sat in front of the Chryslers on the edge of the lawn. The vehicles, along with the five men standing around them, were all ready to depart from The Herm. Unbeknownst to Luther, beneath the hotel five of his men had already departed.

In the front passenger seat of the Studebaker the boss was losing his patience. His leg tapped the floorboard relentlessly. The cigarette between his fingers was burned down to his knuckles. He inhaled one last time and blew smoke out of his scar, then stomped out the butt with his right shoe.

From behind the steering wheel, Wallace checked his watch. "The reception starts in three minutes," the worm said. "We should go."

"The wedding reception will go on for hours," Luther responded. "I'm not worried about missing it. What I *am* worried about is five of my men killing time playing Marco Polo in the basement."

"Alonzo is probably enjoying himself," Wallace suggested.

206

"I *understand* that, but how long could it take?" Luther opened the car door and stepped onto the grass. "At the very least, Owen should have come back and informed me of what the delay is. Very unlike him."

Luther began to feel uneasy. *It's the opium*, he told himself. *Too much or not enough.* He knew deep down that it was something else. In the bowels of The Hermann Hotel, something had gone terribly wrong.

Luther walked over to Nicky. "I want the crate placed in the back of the Kettle. It will be safer there."

"You want the gas to ride with you, boss?" Nicky replied.

Luther smacked Nicky on the side of the head. "Yes, big mouth. The *crate*. Put the *crate* in the Kettle, now!"

"Yes, boss." Nicky removed the box filled with homemade mustard gas canisters from the back of the brown Chrysler and waddled it over to the Kettle's rear.

"I want weapons where they are accessible. Something isn't right." Luther turned to another one of his men. "Head down to the basement and find out what the fucking hold-up is. Keep your heater out when you get to the stairs."

"You got it, boss." The mobster unholstered his handgun and walked back through the main entrance.

"Shit has flown into the fan, I tell ya. I can taste it," the boss said with his lisp. "It's either hit the fan already or it's about to."

~

In the long corridor I reacquainted myself with the Tommy gun, the Colt 1911, and Owen's small revolver. I stuffed the pistols into my pants and made my way down the hallway with the machine gun aimed forward. The back door of the speakeasy was ajar, I entered, gun first, and was met by a woman's scream. "It's all right! Get back!" I hollered at the small crowd. "Please, get back!"

They parted like the red sea and I ran for the speakeasy's iron door. I greeted the first few steps two at a time. Once on the landing, I noticed the shadow of a man at the top of the next flight. I wheeled around the railing and brought the Tommy gun to my shoulder. It was one of Irvin's boys with a pistol pointed at me. I raised the machine gun and sent a burst of .45s into his chest.

He shouldn't have hesitated.

I ascended to the ground floor and stepped over his body. I was sure there wasn't enough time to go around the outside of The Herm and conduct an ambush. I went right and sprinted into the ballroom. The guests who weren't passed out on tables, chairs, and the floor screamed at the sight of me hauling ass. I'll admit that the image of a bloody man wielding a chopper isn't exactly what you hope to see when awakening with a brutal hangover. I couldn't feel bad for them, though. I was in worse shape than all of them combined. I barreled left into the main lobby and collided with Hames, nearly knocking both of us to the carpet.

"Mr. Roane! What in heaven's name is going on? People have heard gunfire! *I've* heard gunfire!"

"Hames, call the police now!"

"You're hurt!"

"I'm fine. Your tux isn't."

"Why do you have a *machine* gun?"

"'Cause I'm in the middle of something! For Christ sakes call the cops and make sure everyone stays in their rooms! Do it, Hames!"

"Yes, yes, Mr. Roane!"

I spotted Luther and his men standing outside in the loop of The Hermann's driveway. "Son of a bitch!" I rasped and ran out of the hotel, locking eyes with the fiend. His disfigured face wore the look of a man who just glimpsed a ghost in the worst possible way. I clenched my teeth and opened fire. The Thompson vibrated against my shoulder. Rounds peppered their way into the mobster's vehicles and kicked up dirt into baby clouds. The men scattered for cover, running into each other as they ducked behind cars.

Wallace fidgeted behind the wheel of the hideous Studebaker, his body exposed via the open passenger door. I took aim and squeezed a burst at him. The worm managed to lean over and close the hatch in the nick of time; fire from the Thompson bounced off the armor-plated door. From behind the Studebaker Luther crawled out of sight. "It's Roane! He got out! I want him dead! Someone put a fucking bullet in him!"

Behind the cover of the brown Chrysler, Nicky opened a door and pulled a cello case onto the ground. He flipped it open and handed the B.A.R. to the man beside him, reserving the Tommy gun for himself. The weapons were already loaded. They cocked the bolts of each machine gun, aimed in my direction, and unleashed a swarm of bullets. A handful of bystanders dove behind hedges while a middle-aged couple held their hands over their ears near a long black Cadillac, both of them confused and screaming. I sprinted at them and tackled the couple to the ground, hooking one in each of my arms. Bullets zipped through the air above us, breaking the Cadillac's glass and pinging into metal. The B.A.R.'s .30-06 rounds cut through the body of the large car. Our cover was quickly being turned into Swiss cheese. "Get behind the engine block!" I pushed them. "Down behind the engine!"

I rolled to one of the rear tires and from a prone position fired sideways underneath the Caddy. A long stream of slugs from my Thompson pushed Nicky and the other man back behind the darker Chrysler. As the B.A.R.-man reloaded, Nicky popped up again and fired at the tire I lay behind, popping it. Air hissed out of it like a cat caught in the crossfire. I stood and aimed the Tommy gun through one of the broken windows. The barrage pushed Nicky back down behind the car as pieces of glass and seat cushions flew at him.

In the back seat of the Studebaker, beside the crate of lethal gas, Irvin frantically flung open another instrument case and armed himself with a semi-automatic Mondragon rifle. He cocked the long weapon and peeked around the back of the armored car. Luther cracked off round after round, each barely missing my head. Gunshots echoed over the property and slammed into my cover. I shrank back down to avoid the drilling of lead.

When shots from the Mondragon slowed down, I returned fire at Luther's position until the Thompson in my hands was empty. Both Luther and I began reloading while Nicky and the man at his side hosed the Cadillac again with automatic fire. I discarded the empty drum from the Tommy gun and jammed the stick magazine into the port, then cocked the machine with my head down, praying.

Luther opened up the driver's door of the salmon-colored piece of shit he used as a car and began shouting at the crouched worm. "Wallace, get this fucking Kettle moving! We gotta get the hell out of here, dammit!"

Wallace turned the ignition. The Studebaker wouldn't start.

"C'mon, dammit!" Shrieked Luther.

"I'm trying, sir." Wallace tried again and the engine failed to comply.

"Don't be a candy ass, Wallace! Put your back into it!"

The worm tried again and again. "It's just not turning over, Luther!"

A bullet's path made for a perfect peephole, allowing me to

see through part of the Cadillac. From the tiny opening I noticed the B.A.R.- wielding mobster foolishly exposing half of his body near the grill of the brown Chrysler. I seized the opportunity and raked lead up the front of his torso. He bent backwards in a bloody mess.

Wallace remained low in the front seat of the Studebaker, fighting his own personal fight against the armored car's starter. Luther watched as one of his men bled out expeditiously on the gravel. The strongest weapon in his arsenal was now unmanned. The boss was losing his nerve. "Do something, Wallace! You're gonna get us killed!"

"I'm trying!" Wallace smacked the car with his palm repeatedly, his glasses slipping out of place and down his nose. With a mind of its own, the Kettle decided to awaken.

"Yes, dammit!" Luther exclaimed.

Wallace turned his attention to a clutch that decided to jam. The boss leaned out from behind the Kettle and shot at me again. I returned fire, spraying dirt into his face. "Shit!" Luther hollered and sank back behind the car to clear his eyes.

In one quick squeeze Nicky threw a handful of .45s from his Thompson, causing me to retreat. He ran empty and dropped an ammo drum to his feet, instantly replacing it with another drum from the cello case. He sprang up like a mole, pulling the bolt back and looking for me to reveal myself. I had the wise-guy in my sights, when the Tommy gun in my hands clicked dry. Nicky witnessed this and gained confidence.

"Ohh, I gotcha in a noose now!" Nicky's voice pitched high.

The meatball of a man came around the back bumper of his cover and lit up the Caddy with burst after burst. He walked out in the open, firing at me as more and more of my body came into his view. I pulled the Colt 1911 from my pants and waited for a clear shot.

I heard a sudden roar, not of gunfire, but of an engine. A yellow Rolls Royce convertible coupe came backing out of the tree line and continued reversing into the driveway. It struck Nicky below the waist, pinning his legs against the Chrysler. The mobster squealed as his bones broke between the two cars.

The driver of the Rolls had hair that almost matched the car's paint job – it was Maude. Her foot remained on the gas, spinning the wheels in place and spraying pebbles towards the front of the car. The wheels dug deeper into the driveway while the trunk of the car pancaked a pain-filled Nicky. I watched him suppress the agony long enough to lift his Tommy gun to the back window of the Rolls.

I cried out desperately, "Maude, get on the floor!"

She looked at me with horror flashing across her face.

"Get on the floor, Maude! *Now!*"

Her head disappeared below the window. Nicky pulled the trigger and held it there, shredding the seats of Maude's car and showering her with broken glass.

She screamed from below the dashboard, her body cramped into a fetal position. Fire exploded from the barrel of Nicky's Thompson ceaselessly until his rounds were depleted. He ejected the drum and felt inside his coat for another. I peered over the Cadillac's window at Luther's car. The boss was still hiding behind the tire, his bookie counterpart locked in an ongoing wrestling match with the clutch.

Nicky fumbled with the last drum of ammo. He managed to reload, but I was already upon him with the 1911. The squatty goon, a total wreck, glared at me and pulled the machine gun's bolt back. "Fuck you, Roane! You ain't nottin'! You ain't nott –" I popped him twice in the chest at close range. Nicky slumped over the trunk of Maude's Rolls, his breathing evanescent.

To my right a rifle round whizzed through the air and smashed the only intact headlight on the brown Chrysler. Luther had regained his vision and dispatched another barrage from the Mondragon. I dropped below the engine as bullets shanked into the vehicle. I glanced at the Colt 1911 in my hand, saw its slide locked back, and threw it away. Nicky's fully loaded Thompson hung from his arm beside me. I liberated the machine gun from him and repaid fire, persuading Luther into a retreat behind his Kettle, which was now lurching away in a starting and stopping motion that was akin to a broken toy. The Mondragon ran empty and the boss tossed it in the back seat of the Studebaker before diving in himself.

The ugly vehicle continued in an inconsistent and somewhat comical motion. Nevertheless, it was *moving* – escaping. In the Kettle's back seat Luther loaded a strip of 9mm slugs into his Mauser C96 pistol.

"Get us out of the driveway, Wallace!"

Wallace nodded nervously, mislaying his spectacles even more. Operating machinery under duress just wasn't his forte. The armored car's tires ploughed the lawn, spewing dirt and grass behind it.

"Is he dead?" Maude's muffled voice came from deep within the Rolls Royce. I assumed she was talking about Nicky.

"Yes," I said. "He's about as dead as Julius Caesar." I opened the door and found her still on the floor, practically under the seat. One of her arms had a small laceration from falling glass.

"You're all right, Maude? You're not hit?"

"Just a scratch, just a scratch," she repeated, her voice fluttering.

I grabbed her by the wrist and helped her out of the car. She stood and fell forward in my arms. From over my shoulder, she could see the Studebaker jerking towards the street.

"He's getting away!" Maude exclaimed.

"With that hunk of metal he won't go very far or very fast."

"What is that *thing?*"

"It's some sort of armored car," I said. "I'm gonna need something stronger to stop it."

I scrutinized the dead man on the opposite side of the Chrysler and the Browning Automatic Rifle that lay next to him. I dashed over to the heavy weapon, found a fresh twenty-round magazine in the cello case, and swapped it out.

"Stay here. See if anyone is injured. Wait for the police," I said to Maude.

Maude replied, "Take my car."

"It will be in worse shape than it already is after I get through with it. It ain't comin' back in one piece," I told her.

"I want *you* back in one piece. Never mind the car."

I placed both machine guns on the front seat of the yellow Rolls Royce and climbed in beside them.

"Stop him, Emmett," she said.

I cut the wheel hard. My foot pressed the pedal to the floor as I worked the clutch. The Rolls sped out between parked cars and Nicky's lifeless body dropped to the dirt. With a cloud of dust behind me I was in pursuit, keeping one hand on the wheel as I used the Thompson to clear away the remaining glass of the destroyed windshield. *Nice set of wheels before today,* I thought. The Rolls skidded out onto the long, straight road and buzzed forward like some colossal antagonized wasp. The Kettle lumbered away from me at an embarrassing pace.

"He's on us, dammit!" Luther shouted from the back seat.

He opened a window and began firing his Mauser C96 at me; each muzzle flash was instantly followed by a ping against the front of the Rolls. I accelerated to close the distance between us.

My right hand lifted the Tommy gun to the absent windshield and rested the weapon's fore grip on the dashboard. I sent a burst at one of the Kettle's wheels and up the back of the car. The .45s bounced off the tires and rear glass. Luther pulled his arm back inside and closed the window.

He reloaded the Mauser, repositioning himself at the Studebaker's thick back window. Luther poked the pistol's thin barrel out of the rear gun port and fired at my head. I ducked below the steering column, driving blindly with my foot flat on the gas. 9mm rounds skipped off the hood of the Rolls and passed over my scalp. I picked up speed and rammed the back of the Kettle, knocking Luther out of his seat. The boss glanced anxiously at the crate of mustard gas as it bounced around heedlessly next to him. I let loose another volley from the Tommy gun, this time from only a car's length away. The consecutive blast cracked the rear window.

Luther lowered his body and reloaded again. "Step on it, Wallace!"

Wallace claimed, "This is the vehicle's top speed!"

I was a one-man band: steering, clutching, shifting, and aiming the Thompson when necessary. At the brief junctures when I neglected the shifter the Rolls would whine for attention. I realized that bullets weren't enough; the Kettle needed to be pushed off the road. I steered left into the opposing lane of traffic and slammed the right side of the Rolls into the Studebaker's running board repeatedly until its robust wheels bumped onto the sidewalk. One more solid connection and the Kettle would meet a tree head on. Luther shot at me through one of the side gun ports, exhausting his ammunition and sending lead jouncing around the interior of the Rolls Royce. Wallace swung the wheel left and clobbered me with a force I couldn't match. The Kettle's weight made it a wrecking ball.

The Rolls was forced back into the other lane and into the path of an oncoming car. Its driver laid on the horn and I swerved hard to the left. I avoided the collision by an inch, the oncoming vehicle's wheels safely passing between the Rolls and the mobster's carriage. The yellow automobile that was once a luxury car couldn't take much more. I had to do something before the Rolls decided to quit on me. I steered the car back into the side of the Studebaker as swiftly as I could and raised the Thompson to Wallace's face. I aimed at a drop of sweat below his glasses. The final foray from the Tommy gun still couldn't break the glass but did manage to rattle the driver. Wallace clung to the steering wheel while almost stripping the gears.

I dropped the Thompson to the floor, allowing the B.A.R. to take the stage. Its bullets, I knew, were strong enough at such a close range to kill the Kettle's tires, but I couldn't get a clear shot at the wheels with the passenger door in the way. With my right hand I opened the door and let it swing out. I accelerated so that the front half of the Rolls was past the gangster's car, slammed on the brakes, and watched as the Kettle's fender ripped the door completely from its hinges. I now had the line of sight I needed.

My hand wrapped around the B.A.R., its long, heavy barrel sitting across the seat to my right. I squeezed out two long bursts, one into each massive tire. The Kettle's front and rear wheels on the driver's side exploded, blowing fragments of rubber all over the street. As the Kettle dipped to one side, I rammed it once more, this time at the dorsal, pushing it into an out-of-control tailspin. Both of our vehicles went whirling wildly down the road as though we were part of some motorized ballet.

The Studebaker flipped over twice before coming to rest. I grappled with the steering wheel and lost. The Rolls jumped the curb and slammed head-on into a light post. My forehead smacked the steering wheel. My eyes closed and the show stopped without applause. I could only hope for an encore.

Eyes opened, closed, and open again. My neck was stiff. I could hear the hissing of deceased engines and police sirens in the distance. Blood was leaking down my face from yet another opening. The top half of the steering wheel stared back at me like a blackened frown. I touched my head; the pain was mind splitting. I looked at the gangster's overturned vehicle. A pair of feet kicked desperately at one of the rear doors. Yellow gas filled the flipped Studebaker. It had been set off in the crash.

Funny how much it resembled an actual kettle now, its nose up in the air, steaming, its contents being brewed. Luther Irvin kicked open the back door, his legs squirming onto the road as he exited his beloved car. The mustard gas had entered him. He coughed unremittingly, gasping between attacks. I could see Wallace now, upside down, dead from the crash or the gas or both.

Luther rolled away from the door. His skin was red and blistered. In his right hand he held my .38 Smith & Wesson. I remembered Owen's compact revolver and felt for it on my waist. It was gone. I searched the inside of the car through vision that burned and flickered similar to an over-exposed film. The pistol had been tossed from the car during the impact. I spotted it in the street.

I opened the door and fell out of the Rolls Royce. I couldn't walk, so I crawled towards the gun. My body dragged against the cold pavement an inch at a time.

Luther came to his feet, coughing, choking, and wavering as though he was already inhaling fumes from hell. The pistol still seemed so far away. He raised my .38 and aimed unsteadily at my helpless figure. He pulled the trigger and was met with a click. He squeezed again; another click, another empty chamber. The hammer rose and before it could fall a third time, Luther collapsed to his knees. My gun dropped from his hand. The mustard gas took him. The mobster fell face first with poison chasing the life from his body. The creator killed by his creation. His solution became mine in that moment.

I still couldn't move. The world around me was a silent movie with no one left on screen: black and white, no subtitles. There was an ending, however, and I found myself accepting it. It swept over me like a warm blanket. I wasn't cold anymore. I just wasn't cold.

# 20.

Whiteness. The walls were white; the floors and ceilings were too, or almost white. Beds and pillows and curtains were white. Everything, everywhere, white and bright. I was laying down. I was waking up. A woman held my hand.

"Am I in heaven?" I asked.

"Depends on what you consider to be heaven," she responded.

I could feel her fingers interlaced with mine, but I couldn't see her.

"I rather hope you aren't in heaven, Emmett. That would mean that I'm dead too… and I'm very much alive."

"Maude?"

"Yes."

My vision cleared and I could see her now. She looked at me from a chair beside the bed. She appeared different without makeup, yet, in a way, more exquisite. Her lips were still a deep red, her eyes still that of a cat, but one that was no longer lost.

"I'm sorry about your car," I said.

"It was my boyfriend's Rolls Royce, so to hell with it."

"He still your boyfriend?"

"Not anymore," she smiled.

"How… how long have I been out for?"

"Almost twenty-four hours," Maude said. "Hit your noggin pretty good out on Bellevue Ave. Gave you a concussion. Doctors were worried about your brain swelling but that didn't happen. Other than that, you have an impressive amount of cuts and bruises. You'll live."

"How long have you been here?"

"Basically the entire time. Waiting for you to come back. The police have been coming by every couple of hours to see if you're awake. I told them the whole story, as did Hames from the hotel, but I suppose they want to hear it from you. They are actually pretty happy you did what you did. Luther Irvin and his group have been giving them problems for years, all over Rhode Island. And now, thanks to you, they are all dead."

"Somebody had to do it," I said. "Everyone is all right at The Hermann? No one took any strays?"

"Nope, not to my knowledge."

"Amazing."

"Yes, it is," she said.

I touched my forehead gently and felt a bandage. "I was actually having a pretty good weekend up until I met you." I smirked at her.

"Me, too, wiseass."

"So today is Monday?"

"Yes, last time I checked," Maude answered.

"I hate Mondays. Are you gonna stay here and feed me?"

"Don't push your luck any more than you already have, Emmett."

We both laughed. It hurt my head but I couldn't help it.

Maude stayed with me the rest of the day. She actually did feed me a little bit; I didn't have to push my luck too hard. Doctors and nurses came in and out about three thousand times, poking me like I was a newly discovered species, or maybe one that was thought to have been extinct. Maude gathered my things from The Herm and placed them on a table in the room. I longed to clothe myself and walk around, but I was still too weak to move. I needed another day in bed.

The police resurfaced and talked to me for about an hour. They told me how they found me face down on Bellevue Avenue, unconscious. They described how they found all the departed mobsters, including the one floating below the cliff walk and another in the tan Chrysler's trunk. They informed me of the letter they found in Luther Irvin's inside pocket, the same one Maude and I tried to hand off to Frank Norelli at the Harvest Festival Ball. The mustard gas had burned itself out by the time the police arrived on the scene; the vast majority of it was contained inside the Kettle, preventing it from spreading. Thankfully, only one of the canisters had been detonated in the rollover.

Before they exited my hospital room five cops shook my hand and thanked me. A Sergeant by the name of Murphy paused at the door and turned back to me. He was a heavy man, graying, with a mustache.

"Oh, and Mr. Roane... that .38 we found in Luther Irvin's hand? It was loaded with only one bullet. Had he pulled that trigger again, the hammer would have landed on it."

I stared at him blankly, realizing right then just how close I had come to never waking up at all, or at least waking up someplace *much* farther away.

"You're lucky, son," The Sergeant said to me.

"I guess I am."

"A guy like you... you should have been a cop," Murphy said.

"Nahh... I don't have the patience. Besides, I'm too much trouble," I smiled.

"The best kind." Murphy tipped his hat and walked away.

After he left I asked Maude to bring the telephone closer. I had the operator place a call to Brian back in Brooklyn and told him what happened. At first he didn't believe me. He finally figured out I wasn't pulling his leg and erupted through the receiver. When he was done yelling at me, he told me he would be in Newport tomorrow. Another friend of ours would make the long trip and drop Brian off at The Hermann. Brian would fetch my Ford Model T and drive us both back to New York.

It was getting late. Maude and I listened to the radio as Paul Whiteman's "Three O'clock in the Morning" came on. We gazed at each other quietly, more being said in those long silent moments than was spoken the entire weekend.

"I'll stay the night with you," Maude finally purred out loud.

"You don't have to."

"I want to. I'll be gone when you wake up, though, I'm going to my mother's. She's sending a car that will be here at dawn."

"Where does your mother live?" I whispered.

"New York. She lives in Manhattan now. I guess I won't be so far from you after all."

"Good, You still owe me a slow dance."

"Find me when you get home. I'll save you a dance."

"Promise?"

"Yes."

The nurse brought in a spare cot and Maude laid down next to me. She ran her finger over the old scar on the side of my head and kissed me, the moonlight acting as a silver frame to us, a frame to a painted memory. A painting that is mostly white but is truthfully so many colors.

"And look now," Maude said, "how hard you have fallen for a heartless girl."

"I think from now on, I'll always fall where I know the landing won't be soft," I said. "That way I know I'll wake up."

We grinned back and forth, sideways and together. My arm stretched out to hers, creating a bridge between us. The second I closed my eyes I was asleep.

Tuesday morning came and Maude was gone. Only her imprint on the bed and a hint of her scent remained. On the small table near my head I noticed a strange shape. A paper airplane sat beside the lamp. On it an address was written, punctuated by a mark made by rosy red lips.

There was a knock on the ajar door. Brian walked inside and took off his hat. He said nothing until he sat down on the edge of Maude's cot.

"Good morning," Brian spoke. "You look like hell."

"You should see the other guys."

"I heard. Not just from you, either. I was chatting up a nurse on the way in here. Apparently you're some kind of local hero. You come here for one weekend and you become a fucking legend."

"I'm not a hero. I'm no legend either. I'm just a guy who wants to go home."

"Don't they want you to stay till the end of the week?"

"Yeah, but I've decided we are leaving in about five minutes. I'm sick of not moving, sick of this food, and goddamn sick of hospitals."

"I think you're just sick in general," Brian sassed. "Mostly mentally."

"Not anymore I ain't. I see you haven't lost your charm, asshole."

"Never. I can't let you go anywhere anymore, you know. And why is there a spare bed in here?"

"I had a friend stay over last night."

"A guy?"

"No, you fairy. A dame, and a top shelf one at that." I sat up in the bed.

"No shit?"

"I shit you not. Now help me up so we can begin my escape."

Brian took my arms and pulled me to my feet. I took baby steps and worked the blood back into my stagnant limbs.

"So did you get her in the sack?" he asked.

"None of your bees wax."

"So you did, you dog."

I eventually responded, "Do something useful with yourself and grab my clothes, will ya?"

Brian waited in the hall as I dressed myself and finally felt like a functional human being again. The corner of a stiff rectangular shape poked me from the inside pocket of my suit. I reached inside and pulled out a crisp bundle of twenty-dollar bills adding up to somewhere around a thousand. Tied to the money was a tiny sack filled with five confetti almonds, a popular token given to guests at just about every Italian wedding I had ever been to. A note was tucked within the stack of cash. It read simply, "Thanks – Frank Norelli." I stuffed it all back inside my suit and smirked. *Money for another weekend, perhaps.*

"You ready princess?" Brian said from the doorway.

"Yes," I said, "very." The bandage was still wrapped around my head. I pulled the fedora down low to hide it.

I picked up my suitcase and swiped Maude's paper airplane from the table, tucking it inside my pea coat. Brian and I exited the room and walked down the hospital hallway, both of us trying too hard to be inconspicuous.

"So did you get my car?" I asked.

"No, I walked," he said sarcastically. "Of course I got your car."

"Good, you're driving. Thanks… by the way."

"Don't mention it. So do I get to meet her?"

"Soon," I said.

# Post Script :

In the passenger seat of my Ford, I teeter on the edge of sleep as the wheels rock me into dreams. I see the ocean beyond a bend in the road. "Stop," I say to Brian.

"What?"

"Stop for a second."

He pulls over and looks at me as if I'm either about to urinate myself or be sick.

"I have to do something. Real quick," I tell him.

I get out of the car and open the back door. Inside my suitcase I find the box. Photographs of Anna, of Anna and me. Everything Anna. I take it under my arm and walk over the dunes to the beach. As always, I feel that urge to open it up, but I don't. I don't need to.

I place it in the sand, unburied by a rock. The tide will come and wrap its hand around the box, carrying it away to some infinite place where it always belonged. Memories in an ocean. I don't worry about them slipping away because they are always here. A part of you, Anna, that I will always have.

Back inside my Ford, Brian steers me out of Newport. The leaves are so many colors. Trees hang over the road like a curtain. I roll down the window and the cold breeze tells me that there will be another day.

"You know… Thanksgiving is the day after tomorrow," Brian says.

"That so?" I reply. "Tomorrow and tomorrow and tomorrow…"

Outside of the window, a leaf finds its way into my hand. I wasn't looking for one; it was just there. I can see you catching one, Anna, sitting beside me, smiling that smile. Perhaps this is you saying goodbye. I let the leaf fly from my grasp. It climbs up and away.

Goodbye, Anna, I'll see you again.

Until *someday.*

Emmett Roane will return.